They Watch
And Other Stories

Jean Bruce

Copyright © 2019 Jean Bruce

All rights reserved.

ISBN: 978-1-7333748-0-4

DEDICATION

This and all other books are dedicated to my family, my friends, everyone who has ever believed in me, and you the reader. Love yourself and the world around you, for love's treasure is that it is versatile, infinite, and everywhere.

CONTENTS

	Acknowledgements	i
1	Legend of Jazzer	1
2	Fear and Bravery	8
3	The Spirit Who Sweats Blood	14
4	Mister Burlap	17
5	A Drop of Blood	30
6	My Friend Hiroshi	35
7	They Watch	37
8	Mummy in My Closet	40
9	Girl on the Bus	50
10	It Wasn't A Bear	58

THEY WATCH AND OTHER STORIES

11	The Mosquito Queen	64
12	By the Riverside	74
13	Under the Bed	84
14	Lost in the Woods	95
15	Chasing Nightmares	113
16	They Watch Still	122
17	The Scarecrow and the Lady in Blue	125
18	Night Rider	131
19	The Blind Spot	134
20	They Watch Always	138
	About the Author	142

ACKNOWLEDGMENTS

A special thank you to Quills for being amazing friends and an amazing audience, as well as their guidance and advice. Thank you to those that gave me the space I needed to write and to those that asked questions and were engaged with the stories who gave me the courage to continue. You are all amazing people and I am so lucky to know you.

THE LEGEND OF JAZZER

It was a new mode of transportation. The opening of the subway began with our city's own Ninth Avenue. October 27, 1904 was the birth of a new way to transport underground, away from the eyes of the sun. Stations came and went from many places. Over time, subways became less of a popular way to transport and became abandoned all over the Western Hemisphere.

My friends and I were especially interested in an abandoned tunnel in called the City Hall Station. I came with them for a thesis on ancient urban transportation. They followed me for company while I intended to gather data; my friend Jeff, however, had a different goal in mind.

"Haven't you heard the stories, guys?" He asked the three of us. Archimedes, a mousy freshman who enjoyed history and not much else, stood closest to me. Rebecca glared at Jeff, chewing her gum. She had her arms crossed as she was uninterested in our eccentric friend's ghost stories. He seemed to want to take every opportunity he could in order to scare the life out of poor Archimedes. Rebecca did not approve. I was admittedly a little interested, but I didn't want to scare Archimedes. No one answered him, hoping it would discourage him from talking about it. It never worked. I had no idea why we thought it might.

"Come on, this is more than just 'history,' this is *History*!" Jeff implored. He was the first one through the taped off entrance to the underground. His upbeat voice echoed the story throughout the narrow tunnel. "Every abandoned subway has stories of this guy. How can you not be curious!"

I suppose we all were a little curious. We were doing this at night, after all. I tried to convince my friends, and convince myself, it was to avoid getting caught by security. But I've always liked a good horror story. Deep down, I think Rebecca and Archimedes liked them, too. Why else would they volunteer to come when they knew how Jeff would be in places like this? We all had our flashlights and cellphones. I hadn't realized until our descent that our phones might not have service underground.

"As the subway stations became abandoned," Jeff's hauntingly cheerful voice persisted. "There were reports of the white subway, which came and left to unknown locations. It didn't stop at the stations. It just came and went, silent as death."

"Can we not tell spooky stories in an abandoned cave, please?" Archimedes gripped my shirt to have support, in case he lost his footing.

"But even as the subways shut down," Jeff continued. "The sound of rumbling could be heard reverberating through the tunnels. And the sound of a whistle. Like a train."

"Subways don't *have* whistles, Jeff," Rebecca rolled her eyes.

"I know that, it's just what I heard," Jeff insisted. "It adds to the mystery. It means something unnatural is lurking in these abandoned subways. Did you hear about the 'mad conductor' in London? He was this guy who used to work for the subway, but lost his job when his route shut down. Well, he went down there again, for old time's sake, and he came out years later. He was shaking and muttering things. 'white subway,' 'there are no eyes,' that sort of thing. What do you suppose happened to him? And how could he last down there for *years* without food or water?"

"Ghosts?" I chuckled, Rebecca's fuchsia-colored hair flashing in the light of my path. I could feel her critical blue eyes staring down Jeff's back, throwing icicles at his dumb blond head and tan, broad back.

"Exactly Dyana, the ghost subway!"

We make it down the stairs to the subway terminal. I could hear all of us gasp and awe at the sheer architecture. This was more than just a subway. Murals of design bloomed from the ceiling and took over our view. There were old posters and announcements against the wall, everything still in decent shape. Papers were yellowed and wrinkled from the condensation. I heard a distant scurrying of rats. I began to jot notes.

"The lights are still on," Archimedes whispered.

Yes, I noticed that. Though it was still dark, the place was lit with some emergency back-up light. "That's strange," I muttered. "The electric bill should have run out of this place. There shouldn't be any light at all."

Jeff seemed pleased with himself, as though to say 'see? I told you there were ghosts,' as though strange lights were proof of ghosts. "Let's just be happy we're so lucky," I assure the others. I jot down things I notice about the subway. I mention the design; the great care there was for the architecture.

"You know what the old man was singing, when they

incarcerated him?" Jeff's voice had a shift; a sudden twinge of chill that I did not like. "It was an old railway nursery song. Something children would sing during the construction of the railroads. When asked why he sang the song he said, 'to be taken away. You sing to him, he take you away. You play a game, then you gone. 'Cept me. I should be gone, so I sing. So he can take me away.'

"Jeff really, can we just focus on getting the information Dyana needs and then go without having to listen to stories?"

"Why, are you scared?" Jeff mocked Archimedes.

"Lay off, Jeff," Rebecca sneered. "Seriously, there's nothing to be scared of. Ghosts aren't real, anyway." Rebecca looked over to Archimedes and playfully tugged at his short brown ponytail. He turned his head and pushed up his glasses, looking towards her. Rebecca returned his gaze with a smile. "It's all just a story," She assured him.

We found ourselves in one of the subway tunnels past the waiting stations. I had questions fill my mind pertaining to my thesis. How much money was put into this luxurious subway station? Was it this fancy because it was the City Hall station, and why would that make a difference? Then other questions came to me. Was that a whistle I heard?

Rebecca busied herself with looking at all the posters along the walls. Archimedes stayed close to her, looking over the broken snack machines. Jeff stood next to me, overlooking the railway.

"One, two, three hear the whistle blow,
Let everybody hear, let everybody know,
The train is a comin' with its silvery glow,
All aboard the train hear the whistle blow."

"Jeff," My voice echoes through the tunnel and it startles me.

Then I hear it, a whistle, like a distant train. I listen closely. My body trembled, the sound was so haunting, but strangely welcoming. I didn't turn my head, but I felt Archimedes and Rebecca walking up from behind me.

My mind was hazy, the whistle got louder. I felt a mix of excitement and horror. There was also a calmness. The whistle blew again. I felt compelled, like the persistent prodding of a song that has been stuck in your head all day. You want to sing it. You have to sing it.

> *"One, two, three hear the whistle blow,*
> *Let everybody hear, let everybody know,*
> *The train is a comin' with its silvery glow,*
> *All aboard the train hear the whistle blow."*

I heard other voices sing with me. We were singing, the four of us, in unison. There was a light glint coming from my left, but I dare not move my head to see. It came to us instead, in front of me, a white subway train. I hear the noise again. It's soothing; it guides me through the doors of the car. My friends joined me. I knew something was wrong but I didn't feel any desire to fight against it. It was like trying to wake up from a good dream. Just a little longer. I want to see where it goes.

The door shut behind us, and as though it closed off the sound of the whistle, like scissors to a thread, I snapped awake. I turned towards Jeff, Rebecca and Archimedes. Jeff seemed dumbfounded, Rebecca was too shocked to react, and Archimedes was trembling.

"Welcome, welcome!" My breath caught in my throat and I spun around. What I saw before me terrified me; I stepped back between Rebecca and Archimedes.

Only they weren't there anymore. It was just me, and the figure before me. He smiled at me, a gray-toothed grin, his skin white as marble and he almost glowed. 'There are no eyes,' Jeff's voice haunted me. I found myself thinking; It's true, there are no eyes. There aren't even places for eyes. No nose, either, just a white, smooth head with no bumps or sockets, and a smile. The only thing above that ghoulish grin is a hat which is gray with thin white stripes sliding vertically down; It matches his suit, reminds me of an old 20s mobster television show. In his pearl white hand is a cane gray as his smile, except for the bulb which was black as a raven's feather.

These similes come to me: Raven's feathers, pearls; such is the language of nightmares. That's what this guy was; a Nightmare.

"Jazzer's the name, this station's my domain! I got a deal for you kid, a real good deal for you."

"Where are my friends?" My voice came out shaky. It wasn't my intention, I meant to sound demanding. Hopefully intimidating, so he wouldn't know how terrified I was. He knew exactly how terrified I was.

"Already played the game little darling," The creature named Jazzer flashed an even wider grin. "They're already gone."

No, I didn't believe it. I couldn't believe it; this was too surreal. They had to be somewhere else. Safe, I hoped. I could find them, maybe. Save them. But first I had to save myself.

"What game?" I asked. Rather, the words came out of my mouth. I never gave the question consent to escape my lips, and I regretted letting my guard down when I saw his head bend forward slightly. It widened his grin, and made it look more sinister. I thought of the Cheshire cat, but even he would be intimidated by that grin. I felt the subway start moving, and I had to grip one of the bars hanging from the ceiling. The notebook and pen I was writing things down on before fell to the ground, but I didn't dare avert my eyes from Jazzer. I didn't dare pick them up. The pen rolled towards the back of the cart.

"This subway has two destinations. All you have to do is find *your* destination."

The next question was from me. I had allowed my lips to make the words, though they came out with difficulty. "What's the other destination?"

Jazzer swung his cane, and a sickly, pitiless chuckle escaped his gray teeth. He took a step back. "Well it's obvious, isn't it? It's *not* your destination."

The subway jerked and I clutched onto the pole, but Jazzer had disappeared. I could feel the subway moving faster. I looked down to pick up my notebook but it had vanished as quietly as Jazzer did. What could I do? I had to find Rebecca, Archimedes and Jeff. Damn it, Jeff, singing that railroad song! I remembered the whistle. Maybe Jeff didn't have a choice.

I pushed those thoughts from my mind. If Jazzer had them kidnapped, he would have them near the front of the subway, right? I gripped the pole to my right. Pole after pole I stumbled to, working my way to the next cart. They had to be there. They had to be together. 'They're already gone,' I couldn't believe that.

I opened up the door to the car in front of me. I walked in and it was just as empty as the cart I was in before. I kept moving, the next cart was the same. It was silent, save for the sound of the wheels speeding underneath the carts. The ride was smooth, but the speed was terrifying. I could feel it trying to suck me back, suck me to the beginning. I went through eight cars already. How long was this subway?

Just as I began to think that I was condemned to an infinite loop, the subway started to slow down. I was able to run without the use of the poles. Ten cars, fifteen cars, twenty cars. On the twenty-first car, I stopped. No, something was different this time. Gradually, things had started to change. I thought back at what the first cart looked like. It was white and plain, with silver poles and furnished benches. This car was gray, and the paint was peeling. There were no poles. It happened so gradually that I hadn't even noticed. Jazzer stood in my way, before the next cart. "Do you think you've made the right choice? To move forward?"

What did he mean by that? Were my friends not in front of the car? No, he was just trying to scare me. "Let me go," I pleaded. "Let me and my friends go!"

I was trembling. He noticed. I almost stumbled as the train stopped. I saw the door to the side open, and the whistle blew once more. Much louder this time. It was deafening.

I sat up gasping. My panting echoed through the long tunnel. Where was I? It was dark. Did I fall? The floor underneath me was wet and some long metal was stabbing my back. I staggered up to stand. My eyes had to adjust to the sudden darkness. My panting slowed, and I realized that I was still in the subway, on the subway tracks. I walked over to the side and climbed up to the station. I was tired, my legs and head hurt. "Jeff?" I cried. "Rebecca, Archimedes?"

I heard footsteps coming down the tunnel. I went back to where I had been lying before and saw flashlights beaming from it. "She's here!" I heard a voice cry. More footsteps came, and I was greeted with a search party. Jeff, Archimedes and Rebecca were all there, in attendance.

I was overjoyed to see them, but I felt uneasy. Jeff handed me my notebook and pen. "You must have dropped it when we lost you," he said. "You had been gone for weeks."

Weeks? I tried to ask Jeff privately if he remembered the subway train. "No, I don't think I was there," he said. Rebecca and Archimedes, when I asked them, said the same thing.

Could I have hit my head? Did I dream all of it? I was sent home to my parents and my older brother. They were all relieved to see me. They held me and kissed me and cried for me. It didn't feel right. Their hugs and kisses and their words felt different.

Everything looks the same, and everything reacts the same as though it were normal, but for every second of my existence I can't help but feel, 'Something's not right. Something feels different.'

This subway has two destinations; *your* destination, and *not* your destination. This is not my destination. These people, my parents and my brother, my friends, they're all strangers. My life is a stranger. Perhaps my real family is somewhere, waiting for me. Worrying about me. I look through the notebook and it's all my handwriting. I eat my meals and they're all the same meals. I wear my clothes and they're all the same. But they're not mine. Have I gone crazy? I think of the incarcerated man in London. *'You sing to him, he take you away.'* I dare not say anything about it out loud. I don't want to end up like him.

But every so often I go back to the abandoned subway. And every night before I sleep in this strange bed, underneath this strange roof, living a stranger's life, I sing to him. I sing, and I pray for the whistle. I want to go to my destination, to my real destination. Maybe this time, I can go back. I'll choose to go back. Surely then, I'll be home again.

> *"One, two, three hear the whistle blow,*
> *Let everybody hear, let everybody know,*
> *The train is a comin' with its silvery glow,*
> *All aboard the train hear the whistle blow."*

FEAR AND BRAVERY

Fear is one of life's most basic instincts. It keeps those that can feel it safe from harm. It provides a quick escape from danger. Fear is helpful even for fun such as providing tension to a game or providing a thrilling story. Fear, as some would surmise, is a necessary evil. It is the demon in every mind which heightens our senses and sometimes dulls our logic. Fear is something primal, and if not careful, it can make monsters out of men.

He witnessed tribesmen prepare for conquest. He mused to himself as he watched families of their enemy fade from existence. He hummed as the foes of the tribesmen were dehumanized in the warrior's minds. He chortled as the men fancied themselves greater, unaware of the fabrications they had decided to believe. Fear became their excuse, and he loved it. "These mortal creatures are so pitiful," His icy voice taunted. "They blind themselves to succumb to my power because their fragile minds cannot bear to comprehend any realm of complexity. They are more comfortable in my clutches then in the open arms of the unknown."

A small, rhythmic chime approached him from behind. An entity much smaller than him stood at his side, music box in hand. "You have little faith in these mortals, yet you must be aware that we are meant to serve them."

Fear hissed, "Us serve them? These weak creatures will perish within a thousand years, while our entities shall continue for as long as time exists. Do not try to humor me, Bravery. The humans are nothing more important than a passing entertainment."

"I can prove to you that they are strong, Fear." Bravery closed her music box, the pearl surface gleaming in the ether of reality. Black tendrils of night swirl and choke the surface of the music box, the design unsettling, yet when opened the melody remains strong and proud.

"You are a small entity, Bravery. You are barely significant yourself. You believe you can deliver these tribesmen from my grasp? Their minds are so clouded they will never manage to even recognize the sun. Their minds are made up, and like mules they will follow me to their doom." Fear grinned towards the men's fantasies of pillage and conquest. They were slaves to his whim; there was no escape from him.

Bravery shied from Fear's wicked smile, yet remained at his side. "I have faith that it will not take much to combat you, Fear. I will be successful, for the mortals' sake and for yours."

"For my sake?" Fear cackled. "Your delusions are as clouded as the human's. I am far too powerful. I counter, for your sake, I advise you abandon trying."

"I will take this challenge, Fear. You will see the true worth of mortals." Bravery descended to the realm of men as the stars spied on their village. She stroked the heads of the slumbering men, a watchful mother over the children of the land. She happened upon one man, curious and inquisitive, who always second-guessed and challenged the common thoughts of those around him. Bravery set her music box beside his head and opened it. The melody filled the young man's mind, painting for him questions and scenarios to pursue should he gain the courage.

"How insulting," Fear growled. "You expect to dethrone me with one man and your meager music box?"

"When your mind is clouded with terror," Bravery whispered to the sleeping man. "And when you feel the weight of uncertainty on your spine, this music will ease your soul. You cannot hear it, but you will be able to feel it, and with its march, I will be with you."

Dusk lit the sky, and the young man awoke to the drums of war. Today was the day they would conquer the barbaric tribesman. But what made them barbaric, he felt himself ask. He felt almost repulsed by this sudden question and busied himself with his armor.

Spear in hand, he followed the march towards the villain's territory. He imagined how he was going for the glory of his tribe. The enemy was too close to their village, and they were in territory that had resources his family needed. There was no other way to obtain the resources. Or was there?

The young man shook his head. It was too late now to think of peace. The barbarians wouldn't understand such gestures. They were like animals, trouncing around with unfit clothes and exercising strange customs. That was what the elder said.

He began to wonder if the elder may be wrong, but he scolded himself. There was no way the elder could be wrong. Besides, it was too late now. He and the rest of the warriors were near the border now, the village was in sight.

The young man saw the little houses and watched the children playing. The huts looked different, but they were recognizably homes. The children reminded him of his son. No, he could not bear to compare his home with this. Yet if he were truly honest, the resemblances were strikingly distracting. They were here to conquer this land. Again, he reminded himself that it was just too late.

Their chief led the charge. Torches in hand, the tribe rushed forward to the idle village that was taken by surprise. Huts were set on fire. The young warrior's allies cheered and shouted at the frightened villagers. The warrior's ears were numb to the cries of pain, and his eyes were blind to the horror in the villagers. He found himself no longer as a single mortal, but rather a part of a large rampaging monster. The warrior ran with the pack and broke pots and took precious items. He waged through the fire they created and stepped over the bodies they laid onto the ground. He was lost to the hivemind of his tribe's monstrous urges.

All the while, Fear crossed his arms and hummed in satisfaction. "You have done nothing, Bravery. Your power is no match for mine, and as I've said before, the mortals are predictable and pitiful. Admit your defeat."

But Bravery said nothing. She looked on to the young warrior she chose, music box held close to her chest. She waited, looking on to the turmoil the mortals had caused. Her frail, slender fingers trailed the mouth of the pearl white box.

Among the chaos, there was a small boy. The warrior spotted him, and chased him into a flaming hut. Once inside, he dodged a stone plate that was thrown his way. The warrior saw a man about his age, legs shaking, holding another plate as he stood between the villain and his wife and son who cowered in the corner. The warrior tightened the grip on his spear.

Bravery's music box opened. The warrior saw the man and entertained the vision of them switching sides. The warrior stood in fear, home ablaze, his wife and son cowering behind him. It terrified the young warrior, and he tried to push the thought back as he had done many times before, but he forced himself to see the man before him like a mirror. His eyes became clear, and the cries outside became deafening.

The warrior raised a hand, mortified of what he and his comrades had done. He held his hand out to the mirror of himself. To see this man and his family die no longer became a fog of actions blanketed by a strong hateful feeling. The family instead became a symbol of his own family. He wanted to see them survive, even if no others did. But it was too late, wasn't it? These villagers would never trust him.

Bravery's music box remained open. The warrior felt a presence of something within him. Something bold and empowering, though it made him also aware of his fear. This may be treason against his fellow warriors. He would be acting differently than them, and he may lose his comradeship because of it if. He became aware of the consequences if he no longer allowed himself to be swept away into their collective destructive path. Yet somehow, this family seemed more important than that. The warrior held out his hand to the family. "Escape with me."

Fear leaned forward. "What is this foolish man thinking?" Bravery kept her music box open, the small, unobtrusive tune planting itself into the souls of the warrior until the family in the hut began to feel it as well.

"Can you understand me?" The warrior cried. "I'm going to help you escape the village."

The woman shouted something to her husband, and the young boy ran from his mother to clutch his father's shirt. They looked to the warrior whose spear pointed away and hand remained outstretched. The father gently pushed his son back and took the warrior's hand.

The warrior was taken aback at how warm and calloused the father's hand was. It reminded him of his own father. The warrior nodded and led him out the hut. As they moved forward, the son and wife took hands and the son gripped his father's shirt once more.

Among the chaos that Fear and the monsters he created had devised, a warrior with a spear smuggled a man, his wife and his child through the village. Every hut was ablaze. Charred human remains lay petrified on the dirt floor, stripped of their silk and jewelry.

Fear snarled. "You believe this small gesture will change my mind?" As Fear spoke, a fellow warrior crossed the young warrior's path.

"What do you think you're doing?" The fellow warrior demanded. He pointed his spear at the family.

"Let them go," The young warrior pleaded. "Even if we destroy this whole village, I will do whatever I can to make sure this family stays alive."

"Are you turning against your own tribe?" The fellow warrior demanded. It was then that the fellow warrior felt a different sort of terror; the fear of betrayal. He turned his spear to the young warrior. "You weak, disgraceful child."

The young warrior felt his back bristle. His breath caught in his throat, and it was hard for him to swallow. "They are not that different than we are. We don't have to do this."

"Traitor," The fellow warrior shouted. He lunged his spear towards the young warrior's chest, but the young warrior dodged and the blade made contact with his arm. The young warrior held his spear like a shield and made a path for the family to run. The two men who were once comrades fought ruthlessly until they both fell to the ashes mixing red with the charcoal.

"Your hero is slain," Fear grinned.

"And yet part of him lives on," Bravery countered.

At first, Fear laughed. Meanwhile, the family escaped and took refuge with an allied tribe. The son, inspired by the warrior, trained and became strong. He married the chief's daughter and began teaching the children of the village how heroes fight and gain honor. He told the children the story about how his family was saved by an enemy who became a hero. Years passed and the young man's students not only strove to become heroes to defend the weak, but also scholars to learn of other cultures and expand the borders of their minds. Fear witnessed almost helplessly as years became centuries and warriors and scholars became leaders and adventurers. Bravery's frail, timid features became bold and stronger as the realm of the unknown shrank.

One day, Fear stood level with Bravery and sneered. "It seems as though you've bested me. Soon I will become nothing and you will become the most powerful entity."

"You will never be destroyed, Fear. It is not my intention to finish you." Bravery stroked Fear's cheek without flinch or hesitation. "Though it is true that I can overpower you, without you there is no need for me to exist. Fear, let us work hand in hand."

Grudgingly at first, Fear agreed. He took Bravery's hand. "I had been consumed by my own power. Perhaps it is in both of our best interests to work together." For the rest of eternity, Fear and

Bravery stood side by side.

THE SPIRIT WHO SWEATS BLOOD

As the legend is told, there is a spirit of the forest that feeds on the blood of man, as man is the threat of the forest. The spirit is a gruesome thing with gray hair and black eyes, and she smiles to her enemies with a permanent grin. She used to sleep in the largest and tallest tree of the forest. A man named Kijinga traveled to the forest seeking shelter. He came across Damu's tree and said, 'My, what a wonderful tree! It will surely keep me sheltered and warm for many years!' Kijinga takes out his axe and chops the tree once. A voice spirit called out to him, 'Dear child of Maarifa, do not swing your axe here.' Kijinga, astonished by the voice of a spirit, replied to her, 'But this is surely a magnificent tree that will last many years as fire and shelter from the rain. It will ease my life and please my fellow villagers.'

'This area of the forest is my home,' the spirit sighed, 'You cannot take this tree or those around it.' Kijinga, angry for being denied the glorious tree, began chopping it once more. 'Cease and listen to the spirit of the forest!' The spirit implored, but the man continued to chop. The spirit tried to convince Kijinga to leave her home be, but he would not listen even as it grew dark. The spirit's voice became softer the more the tree was through. When Kijinga had almost finished, he stopped for a small break.

'Why?' the spirit cried, 'Why do you not listen to me? Do you not see the pain you are causing?' The voice sobbed as the tree swayed and whined over its new, ragged grin.

'I have no need to listen to you,' Kijinga says, 'The time is passing. We are more adult, and many men have lost the desire to listen to spirits anymore. You have nothing to say to interest me. The village is growing and we need more shelter and wood.'

'Your selfishness has clouded your mind. Your attack on the forest has deformed me. My cries have fallen on ears of corn, not a sign of listening or pity. I promise this to you, allow trees to grow and they will give you shelter. Gather the branches they offer to you and you will have your fire. I beg you one more time; leave this tree as my home and I will return the favor of my gratitude.'

Kijinga who cared not for her pleas picked up his axe. Her desperate bargains angered Kijinga and so he stood and proclaimed, 'As long as there is blood in my veins, I will always do what I please!' He chopped through the ragged grin, the sound of chopping drowning out the tired wails of the forest spirit. With one last mighty chop, the tree fell to the ground and moved the earth. The spirit's voice wailed in anger and torment as the wind blew around Kijinga.

In the dim light, Kijinga saw the figure of the spirit. He saw the spirit's matted hair and human-like figure. She hunched over in agony, wailing her torment. She stopped her cries in an instant, and the air had grown thicker. Slowly, she turned herself toward Kijinga, revealing a dreadful face and smiling a dreadful, ragged smile.

Kijinga Decided to run from the gruesome sight and arrive with other men to bring back the tree in the morning. The spirit was quick and tried to grab him with her deformed hand, twisted as a hook. Unsuccessful in his capture, Kijinga rushed home.

Once he had reached the safety of the village, Kijinga thought back on his close encounter with the beastly spirit. Some of the older kinsman had warned him that he should heed the spirits of the forest, but the younger ones who lost their voice with the forest laughed and congratulated Kijinga. He gathered his friends and told the villagers the story of how he bested a forest spirit. The following dawn some men from the village went to take the tree from the now silent forest. The tree was cut down to make firewood and prepare for shelter. As the tree was being cut down, Kijinga noticed many odd insects in the wood. He looked towards these small creatures that floated like mist, legs long, nose thin as a splinter.

That night, Kijinga and his son sat alone in the comfort of a fire made by the wood of the tree. The strange insects joined them. 'Father,' the young son asked, 'What do you suppose these things are?' He raised his hand to show his father one of the insects. His father replied, 'I do not know, but I don't think I like them much.'

As he spoke these words, many of them came to flight. Every insect swarmed to Kijinga and covered his body. He screamed, trying to shake and swat them all away. His son stood in fear. Behind his father was the spirit, but she was bleeding from her entire body. Each drop of blood made a new insect that swarmed Kijinga. This was the last thing the boy saw before his vision turned red and then black. He no longer heard his father's screams.

The villagers found the boy and his father Kijinga in the grass.

The son explained what he saw though he could no longer see. The villagers told the boy that they heard no cries from him or his father, every scrap of wood from the tree had gone missing, and his father was dry of blood.

The spirit never spoke another word. Since she had learned no human listens to spirits anymore, she keeps her mouth shut. It is sure that if Damu needs more blood, she will come again and take the men who do not believe in her and feed on them for taking whatever they wish and not heeding the words of the forest spirits.

MISTER BURLAP

Dane never thought of himself as a lucky person. Compared to any other College student, he might even confess that he had some of the worse luck ever. He had to work full-time to pay his own way and envied the students that had parents pay for them. Dane had tried to get a book he had written to get published but had been rejected over a hundred times. He got the only dorm room with the broken lock which hadn't been fixed, and he made a habit to never buy anything nice or expensive as it was always either stolen or ruined no longer than three months later.

And yet, as he sat in his Renaissance literature class, he kept sneaking glances toward the broad-shouldered, blonde-haired Matthew. If he were lucky, he would gather the courage to speak to him. He looked down, thinking of the last blunder he had in front of Matthew. How he walked toward him in the cafeteria with two coffees, hoping to entice Matt into having lunch with him. He didn't notice the 'Caution: Spill' sign and fell flat on his back, scalding coffee all over his lap and shirt. Some people laughed, and he only saw Matt get up before Dane hurried out of the cafeteria as fast as he could.

Oh Matt, so intelligent, so beautiful. He was much too good for this world, Dane thought. If only there was a way Dane could be suave enough to ask him to spend time together. Matt had a sticker on his laptop that said 'bravery only lies in the heart of fear,' a famous phrase from a book Dane read three years ago. Matt was an avid participator in class. He always had great things to say. Dane seemed to agree with almost everything Matt said. Dane would sometimes pass Matt in the hallway, laughing with his friends. He had such a wonderful laugh.

Matthew must have felt someone looking at him, because he turned his eyes towards Dane. Dane turned his head down so fast he nearly hit his head on the table. He peeked through his neck-length brunette hair to see if Matt was still looking his way. His sappy heart raced, wondering what color Matt's eyes were. Perhaps he could steal a glance.

As he peeked over, however, he thought he saw someone

behind Matt. The figure was obstructed from his view by the strands of his hair. He could see no expression and the image left almost as fast as it came. The person seemed to be wrapped in something, but it was gone now.

Matt was looking at him.

Dane looked down again, noticing that he had turned his head too far. He felt his face grow hotter. He kept his head down the rest of the class, pretending to write notes until their professor announced that they were done for the day.

Once Dane came into his room, he tossed his book-bag onto his bed and sat at his desk before his laptop. His roommate wasn't in, but that was normal; his roommate had a knack for running around all day and sneaking into his girlfriend Sarah's room at night. Dane loved those two friends of his, but he was certain he wouldn't see his roommate until tomorrow when he'd come in to get ready for classes. Dane opened up his laptop, but before turning on the screen he saw something in its reflection.

He froze to get a good look at it; it was human-shaped, but covered in a burlap sack. Frayed ropes wrapped around its neck, and something was protruding from its stomach. It moved, and it caused Dane to jump. He turned around, grabbing a pen by means to protect himself, but the burlap-sacked figure was gone again. "I'm losing it," Dane muttered. It must have been the stress of school. Finals were next month so that must be it. Despite this being what he told himself, he kept looking back as he browsed the internet until dinner. He didn't feel like going into the cafeteria so instead ate the bag of cheese-flavored chips he had left in his room. He wondered if Matt also went to bed at ten. He probably hung out with friends and would be the sort to be awake until two in the morning. Dane scolded himself for thinking about Matt so much. He was acting like a High-schooler, still he was unable to stop.

Dane took a shower, got into the boxers he slept in, and flopped into his bed. He lightly tossed the backpack off of the bed, deciding he'd get homework done tomorrow, and closed his eyes.

It felt like no time had passed before his eyes snapped back open. Dane blinked a few times, trying to get his eyes adjusted to the darkness. He turned his head to his clock, which blared AM 3:00 in blinding red. Strange, what woke him-

'Creeeak'

He shot up from his bed, whipping his head to the door. He

saw the front door was cracked open, but in front of that, dimly illuminated by the hallway light, was the burlap sack man figure.

Dane was too terrified to cry out. It just stood there. Well, the burlap man wasn't even standing. The sack ended in a point, tied closed at the bottom with the same sort of rope that was around its neck, and it almost floated there. It made no noise or movement. The empty canvass of the burlap's face staring at him. The only reason Dane knew which end it was facing was because of the silhouette of the large tongue-like intestine lazily resting where the person's arms seemed to be crossed. Dane blinked hard, patted his face, pinched his arm, but he was awake. And the burlap figure was still there.

There was nothing else Dane could think of to do but just keep staring at it. He didn't dare cry out or close his eyes, or else it might try to come after him. It remained perfectly still. Maybe it was just something in the room that left an image of a man in a burlap sack with a large tongue coming out of its diaphragm?

Like what?

Maybe it was a prank.

"Tyler?" He squeaked. It couldn't possibly be his roommate, but he had to say something; the more silence and stillness that came between the burlap man and him the more terrified Dane felt. There was no movement or response. He didn't know whether to be relieved or not. He braved to speak again, "What do you want from me?"

There was a bang, and a click, and the lights were on. "Whoa! Jeez dude what the fuck?"

The burlap man disappeared the second the light clicked on, and Dane's roommate Tyler filled the space in front of the door. He just walked in to see Dane staring at him in horror. At the sound of his voice, Dane snapped out of something, and looked to Tyler in relief. "I'm sorry, I… Couldn't sleep. I think I'm losing it," Dane confessed.

"Yeah well, don't go all axe-murderer on me man. Alright? You really freaked me out. Do you need to see someone?"

"I… Yeah, I… Maybe I should see the psychiatrist or something."

"Please do, and don't just sit in your bed staring at the door in the dark anymore, you freaked me the fuck out." Regardless, Tyler closed the door and started getting undressed.

"What are you doing here so early?" Dane asked.

"What are you talking about? It's almost eight o' clock in the morning."

Dane turned to look at the time on his clock. AM 7:43, in blaring red numbers.

"Yeah, definitely go see the psych in the nurse's office. Otherwise I'm dragging you there myself."

"I'll go, I'll go." Dane sighed. He shook his head and yawned, rubbing his face to wake him up more. "Maybe it's stress."

"Have you talked to Matt yet? I remember you saying something about that."

Dane blushed. "No I… I meant to, but then I spilled coffee all over myself like an idiot."

"Haha, what? You klutz," Tyler walked to his book-bag and started putting his stuff for chemistry inside. "Do whatever you want Dane, but you only have a month until summer and then who knows what'll happen. I'm not going to spend all of next year listening to you swoon over him with me and Sarah. Just get it over with, man, quick and painless. Isn't that what you told me to do when I wanted to ask out Sarah?"

"That was different," Dane protested. "She liked you from the start. I don't think Matt even knows I exist."

"I don't think it's that different, Tyler protested. However, he dropped the matter. Both of them had classes soon, and they had to get ready.

Matt sat in the row in front of him, diagonal to the left from Dane. This was Intro to Creative writing class; the other class Dane shared with Matt. He avoided eye contact as usual, but for once it wasn't so hard since he was too busy trying to see if the burlap man would show up again. He was preoccupied all throughout class and didn't realize it when class was over until everyone started to stand up and leave. Dane snapped out of his search and joined the crowd. While he was heading to the door, he thought he caught a glimpse of the burlap man through a window.

Just as he turned to look, he bumped into someone. "Ooph," Dane turned back to see who it was.

"Sorry Dane, just forgot my book back in the classroom. You okay?"

Matt stood less than a foot away from Dane, looking right at him. Dane's face grew hot; Matt had green eyes, after all. He cleared his throat. This was not the time to act stupid. "You know my name?"

Matt chuckled lightly. "Yeah, we've had two classes together for the past year. Last semester it was two other English classes, yeah? Is that what you're majoring in?"

"Uh-huh," Dane replied, but then quickly added. "And you?"

"It's a minor," Matt admitted. "I'm actually majoring in Engineering. Strange combination, I know." Matt squeezed past Dane to grab his book. "Anyway, I have a class to go to. Good talking to you."

Dane blurted out, "Yeah, you too." Just like that, Matt was gone. "Oh, my Almighty. I just had a conversation with Matt." Dane felt his heart summer-salting in his chest. He wanted to sing or cry out, but had enough mind to not do so in a classroom doorway. Besides, he had another issue he had to take care of.

He hurried to see if the psychiatrist was available to talk to today. Knowing his luck, she would be booked all week. He felt a lot better though, thinking about the conversation with Matt over and over again. Did he sound too dorky? Maybe. No, it was just fine. He wished he could have set up a date to talk more or something, but Matt knew his name. Dane felt so thrilled about that, and anyway Dane would have to work the rest of the week. Maybe now that they were able to break the ice, it would be easier to talk to Matt. He couldn't wait to tell someone about it!

As he neared the health center, he noticed something in the distance. It was more than 200 feet away, but he could make out the silhouette of the burlap man.

By the time Dane closed the door to the health center, he was out of breath. He walked over to the schedule to see if he could find a slot, and as luck would have it, she was there making adjustments to the schedule. She turned to see him. "Oh Dane, good afternoon. Have you come here to see me? I just got a call of somebody canceling so I'm free now if you'd like."

"Oh, that's perfect, then," Dane blinked. He was welcomed into the office and was asked if he wanted anything to drink, but he declined. "I think I'm losing my mind," He admitted right away.

"What makes you say that," she asked. She sipped her tea as Dane proceeded to tell her the story about how he's been seeing this burlap sack man with the tongue coming out of his diaphragm for the past two days.

"That is interesting," The psychiatrist replied. "Dane, have you ever had a history of hallucinations before?"

"No ma'am," Dane replied.

"Have you had any recent change in diet or head injuries?"

"Not that I know of," Dane replied again. She was making him feel unsure, but she looked thoughtful. After a bit of silence, she started opening a drawer beside her chair and took out a blank piece of paper and a pencil.

"Try doing this," She offered. "Could you draw for me the thing that you've been seeing? And let me know if you see him in this room when you are drawing."

"That sounds a little unorthodox. Also, I'm not great at drawing."

The psychiatrist nodded lightly, "If you don't feel comfortable doing it, that's alright. But I do think it might help. A lot of times, things are scarier when there's mystery to it. Drawing it out may solidify the image, making it less scary."

"Uh, okay." Dane really didn't want to. He didn't want anything to do with this burlap character, and her explanation didn't make much sense to him. Part of him worried that she wanted Dane to draw it as proof to toss him into some correction facility or loony bin. He couldn't really be mad about it if she did tell someone, he felt about right for a loony bin about now.

Once he was done, it looked like a circle on top of a long oval with a squiggle between the two, a squiggle at the bottom of the oval, and a fat worm-like shape coming out the middle of the oval. As he drew it, he kept searching the room and out the window for the creature, but didn't see it.

"Interesting," the psychiatrist's voice muttered as she watched Dane draw the primitive piece. "I saw something similar to that once. A long time ago."

"Really?" Dane looked up to her, the psychiatrist's eyes were misted over, as though she were retreating to a past memory.

"I had another student six years ago mention something similar to this. She started to see this 'man wrapped in a potato sack with a worm coming out his chest' after she was in a car accident. She had awful luck like that, car accidents and the like. She was hit by lightning twice in her life, and she narrowly escaped death several times. She was always so nervous about everything, because anything could happen to her. She later told me about this image that would randomly show up and it became all she could talk about, yet coincidentally she hadn't had her stroke of bad luck during that time either until..."

Dane felt a lump in her throat. "Until?"

She waved him off. "It's nothing. Point is I remember someone else having seen something like this. Why don't you ah, keep that picture? Just keep it with you, maybe hang it up in your room?"

"Why would I want to keep something like this?"

"Well," the psychiatrist suggested, "There are some times where familiarity often gets rid of the fear. Perhaps if the image becomes familiar, you'll stop seeing him. Come back in a week and tell me if anything gets better."

Dane didn't like the notion of the psychiatrist stopping mid-story. What happened to that girl? Did something happen to a student six years ago? Dane decided to hurry to the library. He was supposed to do homework, but... He could always do that later. This was much more important.

He hung the piece of paper over his laptop. Looking at the messy drawing of the thing that's haunted him for the last two days was not his favorite thing in the world, but the psychiatrist would know what to do in these situations, he figured. Dane turned on his laptop and went through the school webpage to find an archive of students. He didn't really know how to go about finding what might have happened to the student. Nothing might have happened at all. He kept the archive up anyhow. It could be any of these people. It could be someone not in the archive. Still, it was a relief knowing that he wasn't the only one to have this disturbing occurrence. Dane lifted his head and took a moment to look at the picture of the burlap man.

Just then, he heard the door to his bedroom open. Dane jumped, spinning around in his chair, just in time to see Tyler slam the door behind him. Tyler chucked his backpack against the wall behind the bed, and the pack fell with a 'thud' onto his covers. "Unbelievable," Tyler muttered, sitting at his own desk and sighing heavily.

"What's wrong, Tyler?" Dane turned his body to look at his friend. Tyler shook his head. "Just this stupid fight."

"Oh, did you and Sarah have a fight?" Dane asked.

Tyler shook his head, "With my philosophy teacher, man. He was talking about fate versus intended action in class today. We had this big debate and it just became a big argument over the whole class. Some of us thought fate existed and those like me were talking about how fate can't possibly be real because there is a myriad of things that could happen. One kid brought up what happened with Christy Simmons six years ago and-"

"Wait," Dane perked up a little. "Six years, what-what happened six years ago? Who is Christy Simmons?"

"You know, the story with the freak car accident."

"I never heard about that," Dane blinked.

"Oh yeah, a car that was broken down and without wheels somehow got free of its chock and sped down a hill and ran over this girl, Christy Simmons."

"What, what happened to her?" Dane's voice squeaked a little.

"Well of course she died, she had a car run over her," Tyler slapped his hand on the table. "But that's not the point! The point is, things like that don't just happen because of fate, and it bugs me how people can just accept that their lives may be purely fate."

'She had awful luck like that, car accidents and the like. She was hit by lightning twice in her life, and she narrowly escaped death several times.' The words filled up the walls of Dane's mind. It couldn't be the same person, could it? Was Tyler wrong in the idea of fate? He looked to the picture of the burlap man that he now had hung up on his wall.

Days passed, and over time Dane noticed that he was starting to get used to the image of the burlap man. He kept showing up, but not in Dane's bedroom. He did not speak about it to anyone else, and he was too afraid to follow up on Christy Simmons. He was so haunted by the image of the grotesque body which followed him that he forgot to take note on his sudden stroke of luck. The door was fixed so that it would lock, school renovations moved Dane's Renaissance class in a smaller room, and now Matt sat right next to him.

For the next few weeks, he would find himself talking more casually to Matt who was glad to speak with Dane before and after class sessions. Dane noted the burlap man standing right next to the professor as Matt asked Dane if he wanted to have lunch together sometime.

"Wuh-yes, yes!" Dane hissed. Some students turned towards the two which made Dane's ears grow hot, and as the professor turned the burlap man was no longer there. Despite that, Matt asked him out to lunch. Dane was asked out to lunch by Matt, and he said yes! Matt chuckled lightly, that brilliant chuckle, and replied, "Cool. See you noon tomorrow at the caf?"

He calls the cafeteria the 'caf,' so cute. Dane nodded with a wide grin. As a probably unnecessary addition, he gave Matt a thumbs-up and immediately felt ashamed of it. It was hard to focus for the rest of class. He couldn't wait to tell Sarah and Tyler.

He found himself running all the way to Sarah's dorm, which was on the other side of the campus. He knocked fervently and heard voices inside. Sarah opened the door and met with Dane's embrace. "We're going to have lunch tomorrow!" Dane laughed and hopped up and down, which Sarah had to follow suit.

Laughing with him, she inquired, "Who, the three of us?"

"No, me and Matt!" Dane cried. He stopped hopping and held Sarah at arm's length before pumping his fist in triumph. "Sarah all my dreams are coming true."

"You've got some low standards for dreams if a lunch with your crush counts. But hey, I'm proud of you! What are you going to wear?"

"Oh, if I wear something nice won't it be obvious?"

"Exactly," Sarah pressed. "Sweetie, you have to let him know you like him! And you know…"

Dane's eyes trailed upwards as he realized the figure which stood right behind Sarah. The tongue could almost be touching her. He almost didn't hear her words, "I'm pretty sure he likes you too."

Dane's reflex pulled Sarah away from the creature, and they both went stumbling backward. "Whoah, Dane! What's gotten into you?"

"There, do you see it?" Dane pointed to the burlap man, but when Sarah turned around, she didn't make any sudden cry or acknowledgement. "My window?"

She couldn't see it at all. Dane lowered his hand. "Sarah I can't take it anymore. I can't tell Tyler and the counselor will just incarcerate me. I have to confess something to you."

Sarah feigned a gasp. "Are you gay?"

"What? Sarah, I'm trying to be serious here," Dane's shoulders slumped at the sound of her giggle.

"I'm sorry, Dane. Okay, what's up?"

"Listen," Dane looked up at the burlap figure which had still not moved. It was eight feet in front of them. "I've been seeing something; a human body wrapped in a burlap sack, with ropes on its neck and below its feet, and a large tongue where the arms would be crossed, poking out of the bag. I'm going crazy from it; I don't know what to do."

Sarah knew Dane for a long time, and though it was true his luck has been improving she doubted he was serious about this burlap image. It was in jest, on her part. "Well, have you ever considered just asking it to leave you alone?"

Just like that, the burlap sack was gone.

"Huh." Dane blinked and looked towards Sarah. "Well then," he started to say when Sarah's phone started ringing.

"Hold on," Sarah told Dane. She opened her phone. "Yeah mom? What is it?" Sarah was silent for a few seconds, before she started shaking her head. Dane felt a stab of concern when he noticed her cover her mouth, her expression twisted in tears. "No, oh no," she gasped. "Well keep me posted mom, okay? I'll try. Love you." Sarah hung up the phone, her eyes turned toward Dane and she opened her mouth, but no sound came out. She tried again. "My dad had a heart attack. They don't know if he's going to make it. I'm sorry, Dane, can I be alone for a while?"

Dane obliged, but he made sure to call Tyler to keep an eye on her and to tell him if anything comes up. In the grief, Dane forgot to tell Tyler the good news about Matt. Dane walked back to his dorm and became even more unsettled with the fact that he had stopped seeing the burlap man out the corner of his eye.

Dane had trouble sleeping that night, and he kept looking at the picture he drew of the burlap man from his bedside. Dane thought about Matt and how excited he was about the lunch, but he knew now that he shouldn't tell anyone about the burlap man. It may have been foolish to think he had anything to do with Sarah's dad being hospitalized, but for some reason the possibility never left his mind.

When the morning came, he was exhausted and Tyler never came back into the room. Still no burlap man, but Dane was wary of the rest of the day. His morning class canceled, which was a bit fortunate except Matt was in that class so Dane didn't get a chance to talk to him before lunch. He thought of what Sarah said and picked out his nicest shirt and neatest pants to wear. He even made a point to pull up his neck-length hair into a ponytail. His bangs still fell over his face, but he liked the look and decided to keep it.

He met up with Matt and sat across from him. They talked about the readings from class and other things they had in common, and learned new things about each other. He learned that Matt had an allergy to nickel and was eager in his hopeful future as an engineer. Dane mentioned that he wrote small fiction books. "I know," Matt confessed with what Dane thought was a blush. Dane blinked, "But how did you know?" Matt tore absently at the straw wrapper for his drink, and it was halfway to confetti by then. "Whenever we're forced to read out loud you always have such a poetic way of writing. I figured you were some sort of author and found your webpage where you post all your scrap ideas."

"Oh no, I forgot about that." Dane hadn't been on that website in months, it was embarrassing that Matt saw all those rejects. "I'm trying to get a book published, but no luck so far."

"That's cool," Matt smiled, furthering the transformation from straw wrapper to confetti. "I have an uncle in the publishing industry, maybe I can ask him about it."

Dane's eyes looked not at Matt, but just to Matt's left. The figure hovering right over Matt, and yet Matt paid no mind.

Matt continued to speak. "Actually, I would love to help you publish it if I could. I really like your writing. And I also wanted to tell you that I sort of like…"

The burlap man went away, in just a blink of Dane's eye.

"Never mind, I have to go."

Dane looked back at Matt incredulously. "What? Why? Where are you going?"

"I just remembered I have to do something. Nice talking to you Dane, good luck! See you in class Monday?"

"Ah, sure," Dane replied, a loss for words. Was he put off by Dane getting distracted? Was Matt about to confess? And could he really get his uncle to publish his book? Dane wasn't sure, and though he kept telling him there was nothing else it could be he kept his mind on the side of caution. The burlap man was there again.

Dane had to talk to the psychiatrist. Even since he made the picture, he hadn't seen the burlap man in his room. He had the feeling that the psychiatrist might know more than she let on.

Dane took a sick day on Saturday so he could set up an appointment with the psychiatrist that morning. Most school employees didn't work weekends, but this Psychiatrist still had her office open on Saturday mornings, due to popular demand.

"I want you to tell me about the girl who also saw the burlap man," Dane demanded as soon as the psychiatrist was in sight of the building.

"Well, good morning to you as well," the psychiatrist replied. She was still working on unlocking the office door. "Would you like some hot chocolate? We have some cups."

"No, thank you," Dane regained his manners, and his breath. He regretted running all the way here, though actually he didn't want to risk catching sight of the burlap man on the way to see the psychiatrist, so thinking further he didn't regret his breathlessness as much.

She became cryptically quiet until she set her things down by her desk. She went over to sit on the rocking chair across from the one Dane sat on. "Okay, it's been a few weeks," the psychiatrist began. "Catch me up with what's going on."

And so, Dane began his long and detailed explanation of everything that happened. He mentioned not seeing the burlap man in his room anymore, but everywhere else, and just before hearing good news. He mentioned Christy Simmons and what happened after Sarah suggested he tell the burlap man to leave him alone. He noted the psychiatrist's eyebrows raise. "You know something," he claimed at last. Her expression at that moment confirmed it for him.

"I do," she admitted. "But I didn't know it for sure until you came in here. I was hoping that the picture would stop Mr. Burlap from showing up. Mr. Burlap is what Christy called it."

"I was right, then," Dane gasped. "But why wouldn't you just tell me? What do I do to get rid of-?"

"Stop right there," the psychiatrist warned. "I know that the very idea of this burlap man is ludicrous, but I had seen Christy every week, and we tried many different ways on how to be rid of him. I had suggested medication, but they hadn't done anything. I suggested rest, time off, and every other trick a doctor learns for mental illnesses and hallucinations. On a whim, I suggested she draw it for me, and I kept it in my office drawer. She stopped seeing it, but only in my office. I wasn't surprised to hear it stayed out of your room."

"What is it?" Dane asked.

"I don't know, I thought maybe Christy was just hallucinating, but after what happened," she paused, and gave me a gentle, even look. "It seems that as long as it stays with you, your luck remains good. As for the picture, maybe it's just as good, a sort of accepting it with you. But every time Christy tried to tell it to go away, it would for a bit of time but then horrible things happened to her. My guess is that she finally was fed up with it, and wished it gone forever, and that's what happened."

"So, what you're saying that I have to live with this thing following me around, probably for the rest of my life?"

"You could try drawing more pictures and keeping them with you. It seems to be the only thing that worked."

But Dane knew that seeing it was one thing, having lots of pictures around with him was another. Suppose someone saw them and asked him. In the end, his humiliation was stronger than his fear.

It became part of his life. Mr. Burlap, as Dane also started calling him, was around for every successful publish, every good grade, and near the end of the school year, Matt confessed to Dane that he admired him as much as Dane admired Matt. Dane could hardly contain his excitement.

Despite all the success, Dane found it hard to focus or celebrate these moments of good fortune, for in the thrall of the luck there stood a burlap man, its grotesque tongue hanging from its folded arms. Sarah's father got better, but Dane didn't dare speak about the Burlap man to anyone else ever again.

A DROP OF BLOOD

Lunch was always her favorite part of the day. Rhonda got to sit with her four best friends. It was the only time she got to speak with them all day long. She didn't have any classes with them this year and it really annoyed her. Even so, they shared the same lunch period and they got to catch up for those thirty glorious minutes. After she got her lunch, she jumped out of line and went to their usual table near the back of the cafeteria. The other four were already engaged in conversation. Rhonda hurried to sit down.

"I don't find that very scary; I've always felt alright in small spaces," Gina said to Kaitlyn, her voice loud as ever. Gina then flipped her long, wavy brown hair behind her and said, "My greatest fear is being eaten alive."

Mindy, though known more often as Carrot, responded by giggling, "By what? We live in the middle of the city!"

"Hey girls," Rhonda greeted, sitting between Kaitlyn and Jillian, the silent friend in their group. "What's this about being eaten alive?"

Carrot waved back at Rhonda with enthusiasm and rubbed her red-freckled arm. "We're talking about biggest fears. My fear was falling, Kaitlyn is claustrophobic, Gina's is getting eaten alive."

"Well just 'cause we live in the city doesn't mean my fear isn't legit," Gina argued. "There's still cannibals. And birds."

"And mosquitoes," Kaitlyn muttered, her grin widening.

"Ew," Rhonda heard Jillian whisper right before Gina replied. "Yeah, and mosquitoes! Uck, I hate mosquitoes."

"Has anyone else ever noticed how you can't kill them most of the time? You swat at them but it's like they, like, they teleport or something," Carrot said.

"Carrot, just because you can't hit it doesn't mean it teleports. It just means you have shitty aim," Rhonda laughed.

Kaitlyn shook her head, "No, I agree with her. I can't ever hit a mosquito, and if I ever did succeed in killing it, I can never find its body."

Rhonda rolled her eyes. The girls were being ridiculous talking about teleporting mosquitos. "Well, I've killed mosquitoes. I've killed lots of mosquitoes. In fact, I don't think I've ever missed a mosquito in my life."

All four girls looked over at Rhonda. "You had to have missed at least one. You've had mosquito bites before."

"Sure, but I always kill the mosquito afterward," Rhonda replied, feeling proud of herself. "A Teleporting mosquito is stupid. I've never missed a mosquito in my life," she lied. The other girls looked irritated at her, but she just shrugged. She didn't get why they would sometimes insist on stupid topics like ghosts and curses or outlandish legends. Rhonda always prided herself as the friend that brought them back down to earth.

"It's still cool to think about," Jillian offered. "Sometimes talking about paranormal things is fun."

"No, it isn't," Rhonda countered. "It's stupid. I love you girls, but the way you talk about morbid stuff is so dumb. What's so fun about talking about things that don't exist until they scare you? The stuff isn't even scary," Unlike the darkness, Rhonda thought. Without having the ability to see where someone was going or where everything is, that's when things became dangerous.

"Well you know what, Rhonda," Kaitlyn blurted out, resting her plump arms on the table. "Sometimes being scared is fun, and they scare us, so stop being such a nay-sayer about everything."

"I'm not a nay-sayer about everything," Rhonda countered. "Just for stupid things."

Jillian was the one to change the conversation to prevent any tense air. The rest of the day went by like normal, though Rhonda's friends seemed a bit less cheerful than usual.

Later that afternoon, Rhonda was at home studying for Spanish. Her short black hair was still wet from the shower, but she was letting it drip dry for that full and slightly waxy look it had when it was. She didn't think much about the lunch conversation. She was sure the girls would cool off by tomorrow and they could talk again like nothing happened. She was working through the book about adverbs, but then the power went out.

"Mom," Rhonda called out from her room. "What happened?!"

Her mother's voice came from the kitchen, "Your father is looking into it now, Rhonda. It's still daylight, you'll be fine."

Rhonda didn't like the dark, but her mom was right. The sun was setting, but it was still daylight. She strained to look at the pages through her window, but decided that it was enough for one day anyway. Then she saw something out the corner of her eye. "Eugh, a mosquito," She muttered and whacked her arm as fast as she could. She couldn't tell in the light whether she got it or not, but there was no way she didn't. Rhonda got up from her chair and turned to her bed.

She saw the mosquito flying, once more, out the corner of her eye. Rhonda strained to follow it and when it got close enough, she slapped her hands together with the mosquito right between them. She opened her hands to see the mosquito across the room toward her bed.

"Stupid bug," Rhonda muttered. Since she had no power and nothing to do, she made it a goal to teach the blood-sucker a lesson. She grabbed one of her flip-flops. "Last thing I want when I wake up tomorrow morning are mosquito bites." She got closer to it and once it landed on the wall, Rhonda whacked it hard with her flip-flop. She got it this time, feeling a mix of pride and disgust at the dead mosquito on her flip-flop. She went to put it away when she noticed another mosquito by her window.

"How are all these mosquitos getting in? My window is closed." Rhonda went out her bedroom door to find her mom or dad. She saw dad on the phone, talking about the bill to the electric company. Her mom wasn't far, so she went to her. "Mom, mosquitoes keep getting into my room. Did you leave a door or window open somewhere?"

"And let the heat in?" Her mother responded. "You know bugs. They just find a way. Maybe they think you have sweet blood," She joked.

Rhonda wasn't pleased. "Do we have bug spray or anything?"

"Maybe try the bathroom closet," her mom replied before getting up from the kitchen table and walking to the bookshelf for a book. She picked up her battery-operated book lamp and pulled out a book from the shelves. Rhonda sighed and made her way to the bathroom closet. She couldn't find bug spray, but she found ant killer. Figuring this was close enough to kill off any more mosquitoes she comes across, she made her way back into her room.

When she got in her room, there were four or five of them. Rhonda crunched up her nose and stuck out her tongue and then sprayed them in a mist of poison. Rhonda did a once-over her room to make sure she didn't miss any and then she decided to go to bed early before it got too dark. If it had to be dark, at least she'd be asleep for it.

The dream world had a school day prepared for Rhonda. She was in a state of constant recess. The sun was bright and the she was happy. Rhonda stirred from her sleep when she felt something wet on her forehead. She brushed it off and yawned, wanting to keep her eyes closed. She didn't want to open her eyes to see the darkness. She didn't want to not be able to turn on her lights.

Another drop of liquid fell on her nose. The lights of the room blared back on, and Rhonda shut her eyes more. The power must've come back. She wiped at the liquid and rested her hand to her side. She looked at it.

Rhonda's hand had blood smeared on it.

What could be dripping blood?

Out the corner of her eye, she saw something on top of her. She turned her head to it.

The monster's naked body was seeping blood from her pores. She looked at Rhonda with black eyes and tiny white pupils. She had a permanent grin from ear to ear, stapled shut except for the portion that revealed jagged, uneven yellow teeth. Her jet-black hair rested in disarray. Rhonda screamed.

The bleeding woman pushed her hand over Rhonda's mouth. The monster's disfigured, finger-less hand felt as though it wasn't there except Rhonda couldn't manage screaming through it. The woman leaned forward, mosquitoes flew all around the room, many of them going to the light bulb, dimming the light. Rhonda tried to squirm away, but her body was numb and itchy. She felt tears falling from her eyes. No, they weren't tears, it was blood.

Rhonda's vision blurred and turned red, and the mosquitoes covered the last of the light. She could feel the hand over her mouth, but she couldn't see the woman anymore. She couldn't see anything anymore. She was plunged into darkness.

Hours later, a mother and father stood together in horror and disbelief in their missing daughter's room. "I heard screaming," Rhonda's father told the policeman. "I ran into her room to see what happened and she was gone. Her light was on; the power went out yesterday. It came back on in the middle of the night."

Police went through a thorough investigation of Rhonda's room, but there were no signs of struggle. Her Spanish books lay on the desk, her bed was clean of any other DNA besides her own, and nothing was missing from her room.

One officer went to the closet and saw a pair of green flip-flops in front of the door. He moved them carefully to open the closet when he felt something on the back of his neck. He whacked at it and looked at his hand. "Ha, gotcha you damn mosquito."

MY FRIEND HIROSHI

My friend Hiroshi is very funny. He stands upside down and grins all the time. He wears a baseball cap but says he has never played baseball. I asked him if he would like to play with me someday, and he said he would love to if he can find out how to turn over. He found me when I was crying behind the school. He told me from where he was my sad face looked like a laugh. He likes to see me happy, but he is upside-down so he can only see me frown.

My friend Hiroshi is very nice. He watches me play with my toy cars and says that I am a good little boy. My friend Hiroshi tells me lots of things about my friends and family that I didn't know. He says my parents smile all the time. I hear them yelling from my room, but Hiroshi tells me they must be happy because they are always smiling.

My friend Hiroshi is very happy. He sings and plays with me. We play hide-and-seek. He is easy to find, but mom and dad can never find him. I don't think they're looking very hard. His smile is very wide as he always speaks to me, but he is upside-down so he always looks like he is sad.

My friend Hiroshi is careful. He always tells me not to look out my window. He said that bad thoughts wait by the window. He keeps me away from it, and keeps me in my room, away from my smiling parents. Hiroshi tries to make me laugh so loud that even my mom and dad can't be heard.

My friend Hiroshi is very worried. My dad came in to my room and did not play nice. I woke up later after dad left. Hiroshi asked me if I could still see out of my right eye, but I could not shake my head. Hiroshi does not like mom and dad. They never play nice. He tells me again to not look out the window.

My friend Hiroshi will be very mad. Even though he tells me there are bad thoughts by the window, I walk to it when he is not looking. The sky looks different with only one eye. My throat hurts too much to talk, but Hiroshi always knows what I want to say. I wonder sometimes how fun it would be to fly. I want to know how Hiroshi feels always being upside-down. If I hold myself outside my window upside-down, will I start floating like Hiroshi? Then maybe I can smile all the time like he does.

I am sorry, my friend Hiroshi.

THEY WATCH

You will be lucky if you never see them. You walk in your room, shower, drive your car to wherever you need to be, and all the while you are never alone. This may be comforting for some, and I had once read that they are meant to be your eyes when you cannot see. They are creatures that look when you have no ability to look. They lurk and they watch. You are never alone.

In the beginning, I was certain that I was just acting crazy. I suddenly became obsessed with what my brother called 'the eyes of the shadow.' It may have something to do with his death afterword. It happened so bizarrely that I couldn't imagine it being coincidence. My brother was driving to work when a semi swerved into him and forced him off the road, his car ramming into a pole and instantly killing him. The semi driver mentioned having seen, for a split second, eyes staring at him from his passenger's seat. He later admitted it was his shadow that spooked him.

I started looking on to other incidents like these. It was hard at first to find, but after a time the similar occurrences would almost jump out at me. There were many people who were tragically killed due to being spooked by their shadow and each one mentioned having sworn eyes were staring at them, but there never were any eyes when they turned around.

Sometimes I feel the eyes staring at me as well, but I dare not turn to look. I know too well what happens after I've seen them. I will end up like my brother. With the recollection of my brother, and the secluded tales that I have researched, as well as my own theories, I will try to explain these eyes that reside in shadows as best as I can.

They have been there the entire time, in moments when a person is alone. They are careful to not be seen, and they only open their eyes when no one is looking. They always stare at you. Their eyes never leave your person, constantly staring and unblinking. My brother, when he had seen them, mentioned that the eyes he saw seemed crudely drawn and moved like an uneven pencil animation. The eyes had no color or expression, just wide-eyed staring. The eyes were dis-proportioned, with cartoon-ish lashes. The irises had no color, just white. But the whites were much more real than the drawn outline. He saw them only briefly, but they made eye contact. They blackened and closed without a sound.

He was in his shower when he saw them. It may have been lack of oxygen, since my brother loves taking long, hot showers. He called me shortly after and told me he felt scared for his life. He kept staring at his shadow, but the eyes never returned. I told him not to worry. There was no way for me to know that he was correct in thinking he was no longer safe. My brother drove to work in the usual route, when suddenly a semi coming the opposite way swerved right towards him. In a panic, he turned his wheel right and hit a telephone pole head-on.

There was a woman that fell through a window. She was at a friend's party and had climbed a ladder to put up streamers. Someone cried out and knocked the ladder, and it toppled over, through the two-story window onto a chain-link fence. The person that knocked over the ladder, when asked to make a statement, said she thought she saw something on the floor and it startled her. It was something in her shadow, but she didn't get a good look.

Another instance I can recall is the story of the woodsman. A well-known psychiatrist about thirty years back was working on a study about the connections people make mentally between themselves and their shadows. Though it's understood that a shadow is only blocked sunlight by a solid thing, there are those who still make a mental separation between themselves and this absence of light. As he continued his research, he wrote in his memoirs about having noticed something distressing in his own shadow. Looming on the wall, his desk lamp being the only source of light, he noticed two huge bulging eyes staring right down at him over his shoulder. He didn't make eye-contact with it, but knew it had been there.

He was now wary of this matter and tried to convince himself it was a sort of hallucination from too much work, and decided to take a small weekend vacation in the woods. A weekend turned into a week, which became weeks, and a search party went to look for him. His wife bought posters and fliers and media feed to find her missing husband, but it was almost a year until he was found. Snow was melting and it was spring, and a couple women were out hunting. On the side of a bank, they noticed a tattered piece of paper. One woman found more pieces and collected them, the other woman found the journal, and the man holding the journal in his hand. He wasn't quite thawed out from the winter. The journal started as a diary, mentioning again the eyes of the shadow, then the words became infrequent and instead the rest of the pages were filled of blotchy images of his shadow with various eyes. Some images had more than two eyes. In the last few pages, the eyes filled the shadow and lastly the entire paper.

His body was found in a place that had been searched before. His autopsy proved it was starvation that finished his life, four months after his disappearance. His car was waiting full and working at the cabin where he supposedly spent his weekend. Some investigators offer that he may have purposefully been hiding from the search parties. From the journal entries, they suppose it was paranoia.

This phenomenon of individuals noticing these eyes and then perishing through various means led me to my own investigation. I felt I owed it to my brother, who was by no means the sort to lie to anyone. What manner of demon had overtaken him? What sort of spirit would want to steal his shadow as its own? What is the purpose? These are the questions I wanted to answer going into my research. My brother knew I would not think he was crazy, and I do not. I believe there is something else going on with these shadows.

MUMMY IN MY CLOSET

Jenny Wyverson was never much for cleaning. As a child, Jenny was so bad at it that her mother had given up trying to get Jenny to clean her room. She would toss her clothes on the floor, bring food, dishes and canned drinks, throw candy wrappers and old school papers on the floor, and so on. This habit only got worse as she got older, and she would misplace her car keys, her bills, important papers, and as a result she was late for nearly every arrangement.

She never had people over. She would instead visit friends where they were, or go out to eat. She was caring and funny and plenty charming, but her cleaning habits, all her friends agreed, were borderline frustrating. Whenever she wanted to drive her friends, they would refuse because they could hardly find a place to sit in her car. Every seat was littered with garbage.

"I'll tell you what," Jenny was absent-mindedly stirring her drink as she and her dearest friend Francine sat together at a breakfast joint. Francine was the one speaking, the two of them having talked about Jenny's problem before. Jenny always said she would clean before now, but she never did, or she would only pick up a few things before getting distracted. Three years of mess was now all over her house and car and Francine was listening to how Jenny started noticing a lot of flies around her room. "I'll tell you what," Francine stated again. "How about if I come over to help you clean up a little?"

"That won't work, Francine. It's just going to get dirty again," Jenny replied. "No one has to live in my apartment with me, so why should I clean?"

"Well don't you want people to come over? And what about roaches, and bedbugs? If it gets bad enough, it could affect the nearby apartments. They'll cause an uproar. You could get evicted."

"I could just go back and live with my mom," Jenny shrugged.

"So you'd rather go back and live with your mom forever than clean your own damn mess? Come on, Jenny. You're going to get sick in that apartment someday. It's more than just looking nice, it's a matter of health and hygiene. You have to take care of yourself or things will only get worse. You want those flies gone, don't you?"

Jenny couldn't argue with that. She hated flies, and dreamed of a life without flies. Maybe she could, if she would only clean her house or at least the car. "I feel bad asking you to help me, though."

"It's only going to be one day of cleaning," Francine reminded her. "Just to get a taste of what a clean room would feel like. Maybe then you'll start cleaning yourself. Besides, I'm curious to see just how bad the apartment has gotten."

"Oh, so it boils down to morbid curiosity," Jenny laughed. Francine stole a potato wedge in protest.

The girls decided to get together early in the morning later that week. They would spend the whole day cleaning together, Francine as the leader. She brought a bunch of cleaning supplies from her own house and a box of trash bags. When Jenny welcomed her in, Francine didn't even know how to walk through the door. Boxes and books and clothes were piled high in a labyrinth. Every inch of the floor had wrappers and cans at least knee-deep. Francine started to get the fear that there may be an animal living in the garbage. Then just as she suspected, the air was filled with the buzzing of what must have been hundreds of flies. How could one person accumulate this much garbage in three years? "This is," Francine breathed, "A lot worse than I thought."

So they started cleaning. Two hours in and they already threw away about six garbage bags worth of stuff, and they were only just starting to see the floor. Jenny was working on lugging the boxes of her stuff and books to her bedroom so they could get the living room cleaned.

Jenny had a box of stuffed animals she never unpacked after leaving her mother's house when she noticed something peeking out of her closet. At first she shook her head and ignored it.

Three more hours in and the living room was starting to show signs of improvement. With the two girls working together, listening to music and talking and laughing, the time and work flew by. Jenny was starting to enjoy herself, despite the actual task at hand. This time she stepped into her room to hunt for another CD to put into the old boom-box Francine brought with her. They were close to Jenny's own surround sound CD player, but not there yet. The CD was in the closet, she remembered, and she opened the door of her closet after pushing away the pile in front of the door.

The door was heavy, and when the door swung open a bunch

of items fell onto the floor, including what Jenny instantly recognized as a human body. It was wrapped in something but random strands of black hair stuck out from the head, and it made a sickening 'thump' over all her things on the floor. The flies that flew about in her room all swarmed over it. Jenny screamed.

"What, what is it?!" Francine dashed as fast as she could to her friend's room, dropping the broom she had been holding, and only halfway to getting to the room did she realize she should have kept the broom as a sort of weapon in case it was a rat. She didn't have time to correct or think about her mistake because she was already at Jenny's side, staring at what Jenny was staring at.

It was a basketball and a few other items, wrapped around in bed sheets. Jenny stopped screaming as Francine made it to the room.

"Oh, I thought for a minute..." Jenny looked down at the sheets and the basketball. Whatever she saw before seemed to change right before her eyes, but as she could see now it was nothing to be afraid of. She looked at Francine, put a hand to her heart and sighed. "I thought it was a dead body."

The absurdity caused Francine to burst into laughter, "Skeletons in your closet for real, Jenny?"

"More like a mummy," Jenny corrected. But of course, it was just a basketball and sheets. She didn't even know how she could have mixed it up with something like that. The way it fell on the ground seemed so real.

The rest of the day, the two girls managed to clean the entire living room and celebrated with a pizza. They watched a movie together in the now clean room, and Jenny felt comfortable in her space. She considered how nice it would be if all her house was like this, but she knew she was just too lazy. She did want a clean house and a clean car, but not as bad as she wanted to not clean. Maybe if she could convince Francine to come over another day, it was a lot more fun doing it with another person. Jenny thought there was something in her kitchen, and when she looked over, she realized it was only the vacuum and a plate behind it on the wall. For a second she thought it looked like a head and shoulders, and the fabric on the vacuum bag made the flashing light from the movie make it look more like bandages.

Now the bedroom was too messy even to get to her bed, so Jenny slept on her couch instead. It was uncomfortable, but less uncomfortable than her bedroom would be. Besides, late at night she decided that she didn't want to be near her closet. Francine had gone home. Both girls had to work the next day. Jenny felt a little better at work than usual. She thought about how great it was to have Francine over at her place for once. Too bad it wouldn't happen a second time, Jenny knew eventually the room would get bad again. It was nice while it lasted. Her mundane work at the call center made her want to go home to her clean living-room even more.

Once she made it home, she got out of her clothes and into the shower. She imagined washing away the customer service. She was great with people, but having to work for customers really put a perspective in one's life. She thought to herself how much nicer it would be if all the customers just didn't call one day, and Jenny and all the others would get a paid day off. She was in the middle of this thought when some shadow caught her eye at the other side of the curtain.

It was in the shape of a man. Jenny's heart skipped a beat. Did someone come into her house? She was naked in the shower, the most vulnerable place, Jenny believed, to be. She peeked through the curtains and saw her towel hanging and a plate propped on the hanger. A plate? How did that get there? Jenny didn't recall ever bringing a plate into the bathroom or ever propping it up in such a place, but she couldn't recall not doing it, either.

Her house was so messy she didn't even remember where or how she had half of the mess. Relieved it was just a plate and towel; she finished up the shower and took off the plate, then dried off with the towel. "Might as well put this in the kitchen," she said to herself.

Well she couldn't make her way to the sink, but she could make it to the fridge. She opened it to put the plate in there for now only to notice that a bunch of flies were buzzing around the fridge. Had something gone bad? She opened the fridge.

"Aah!" she hollered and fell backwards into the pile of garbage. She stared in horror at the figure of the wrapped-up person in the fridge, its head with strands of greasy black hair falling down its face, kneeling in the fridge, head downturned lightly. Jenny rubbed her eyes, but the figure was still there. No, this was no illusion. The bandages, they looked like strips of meat, but it had goosebumps, like the skin of a chicken. Skin. Was it skin?!

"Eeeeuuugh!" She hollered again, overcome with a horrified disgust. She scrambled to her legs to call the police, but right in front of her eyes, as though a fading mirage, the form began to change. The head of the person became a watermelon, and the body, kneeling forward, was replaced with leftover ham and a case of soda sitting below it. She ran into her living room. The cleanliness of it calmed her down a little. She needed to think about what to do, or even what was happening. She wanted to call Francine but she was at work, and she already got in trouble twice calling Francine at work. All the other friends she could think of wouldn't believe her, or understand. They've never seen her house like Francine had, and anyway, how could she describe a mummy wrapped in flesh that later turns into other stuff?

Maybe if the thing didn't have other stuff to turn into, she would be able to catch it somehow and prove to someone. Or if she could take a picture of it, then she could prove what she's seeing. She didn't know if it would show up in the picture but it was her only shot.

Jenny grabbed the box of bags that Francine left behind and started work on throwing garbage out from the kitchen. She really wanted to get to her room first, but she felt wary about starting in the middle of the mess where the mummy could be anywhere, or be anything. She only got about half of the work done before she was ready to pass out. She had been at it all day since coming home from work. She went back into the living room, tried to see if anything could be construed as a head and body, then with satisfaction she went back to bed.

She woke up late. Frantically, she brushed her teeth and threw on clothes from the floor. She thought she saw the mummy again in the hallway by the bathroom but she didn't have the camera on hand and she didn't have the time to hunt for it. She would likely see it after work, she thought with bitterness. And if she didn't, it would be all the better.

Jenny was distracted at work. She noticed that she didn't have any trouble with the mummy there. In fact, she even found herself looking for things that could be a head and body, but even those things were just objects and never manifested into a mummy wrapped up in flesh. Could it have something to do with her house?

Jenny was exhausted from work, and decided to stop by a fast food place on her way home for some comfort food. She went through the drive-thru and munched on her fries during the drive. On the back road just before the parking lot to her house, she reached for her drink when she noticed something in her rear-view mirror.

It was the mummy, sitting behind the passenger's seat. Its black hair hung over its head, the fleshy bandages uneven and seemed as though it was about to come off. Jenny cried out in horror and disgust, and slammed on the break out of reflex. She stopped the car and turned around.

It was just the back seat, covered in fast food wrappers and clothes. It took a moment for Jenny to calm her heart. "That's it," she said to herself. "I'm cleaning this car!"

So that's what she did for the rest of the day. By the time she was done, the car seemed almost new except for the permanent stains: scars of misuse and neglect. But now her old car was clean, and it almost looked happier. Jenny was relieved in a way, but wary about the mummy, and upset she had lost another day to cleaning. She wanted, or even needed to spend time with her friends, but she had another morning shift the next day. It would have to wait until tomorrow afternoon.

The following morning was the same as the day before. Woke up late, hurried to work, saw the mummy briefly in her hallway and was distracted all throughout the day. Some coworkers asked if she was doing alright, but she only sighed and muttered something about a mess back home. Her coworkers were kind enough to understand, but of course the customers didn't. There really is nothing like working customer service. The only difference was that there was no mummy sighting in her car on the way home. The seat remained a seat, no matter how much she glanced over to it.

She called Matt and Gloria, unaware that they had gone for the weekend to celebrate their anniversary. She tried to call Luke but he was busy with his own trouble. She tried to entice him by saying she cleaned her car. "As much as I'd love to see that," he admitted. "But I really have to fill out these applications. I just can't stand it at work anymore. Maybe tomorrow."

Francine was also at work for a few more hours, so until later that night she kept her camera by her side and started finishing up the kitchen. As she was cleaning, she didn't notice the mummy.

Maybe it was finally gone.

Jenny called the second she could, but Francine didn't answer. She called again. "Gimme a sec, I'm leaving right now," Francine answered. Jenny waited for a few minutes, hearing people on the other end. Probably her clients; Francine worked real-estate and she could have been finishing up with showing someone a house. Francine came back at last. "Okay I can talk. I sold two houses today!"

"That's rad, Francine. We should celebrate!"

"I can't today, Jenny. I'm so wiped out."

Jenny didn't mean to sound desperate. "I really need you with me right now."

"Why, what's wrong?" Francine suddenly sounded alarmed. "Are you okay?"

"I don't know," Jenny admitted. "I've been seeing things. In my house, I keep seeing this... Thing. I don't know, can I meet you somewhere?"

"Sure, okay," Francine replied. "Just come over to my house, I'll start some tea or whatever."

Jenny rushed out of her house, paying the dark hallway and the mess no mind, and drove over to Francine's house. Francine met Jenny in Francine's parking lot. "Whooooah," Francine whistled. "Did you get a new car?"

"Very funny," Jenny bumped her hip with Francine. They looked at the clean car together, and Francine kept crying out 'ooh' and 'aah' as though she had never seen a clean car before. "What brought this on? Was it our cleaning day?" Francine asked.

"Sort of," Jenny rubbed her arms as they were crossed. "Can we go inside now?"

"Sure," Francine led the way into the house where their tea had been cooling. Francine even added a little extra class, dumping Oreo's on a tray for them to share. Francine was concerned, seeing Jenny so frazzled. Usually Jenny was the confident friend. Francine couldn't think of a thing that would bring Jenny down this way. She sat across from her friend at the kitchen table, and took a sip of her tea. Nope, still too hot. She hoped the heat wouldn't burn her tongue too bad. She ignored it, however, more preoccupied with the state of her friend. "Alright, so what did you want to talk about?"

"Okay, I know this is going to sound weird," Jenny started.

"Ever since the day we started cleaning, I keep finding this mummy thing everywhere."

"A mummy thing?" Francine parroted.

"Yeah, wherever there's something with the shape of a head and body. But after a while it changes into just clutter. It's why I've been cleaning, because I haven't been noticing it anywhere else but in my mess in my room."

"Maybe it's your brain telling you that you need to clean more often?"

"Sure, maybe," Jenny admitted. "But this mummy, it's wrapped in flesh."

"Ew, gross! Jenny what the heck?" Francine set down the cookie she was just about to eat.

"It's true though, it's so awful, and really vivid. I don't know what to do."

"Clean your house," Jenny replied. "It seems obvious."

"I've spent three days straight working and cleaning," Jenny sighed. "What if it's all clean and I still see the mummy? What am I supposed to do then?"

"Well, you won't know until you try, right?"

"I love how you're not questioning my sanity with this whole hallucinating-a-mummy thing."

"Oh Jen," Francine laughed. "I already knew you were crazy. This is what friends are for. Just make sure to talk to me whenever things get worse, okay? I'm here for you."

"Thanks, Fran," Jenny smiled. She felt a lot better being there with Francine. She made it a lot easier to talk to. She didn't even question Jenny's possible mental break down, she just took it in stride. She fancied this was what true friendship must be.

"Next time we both have a day off," Francine offered. "I'll come and help out again."

"Are you just interested in how far I get by myself in a week?" Jenny asked.

"A little," Francine admitted.

It would be four more days until Francine could come and help with the cleaning. In the meantime, Jenny underestimated how on-edge she would feel being in her own house. She started sleeping with the lights on, because she could see the mummy more often in the dark. It gave her headaches, and the couch was starting to make her back hurt. She managed to clean the bathroom and the kitchen, and she kept her car and living room clean. A few times she tried to catch the creature on her camera, but every time just as the camera clicked, the mummy would flash into whatever items it pleased. To her horror, the being came in many sizes. Once it had been in her sock drawer, just about the size of the palm of her hand. She tried to hit it, hoping she could kill it somehow. But they were only socks.

Francine arrived not a minute later than eight in the morning. She was surprised to learn that Jenny had little sleep over the past couple days and she looked as though she never rested. But the house looked great, with exception to her bedroom. It looked like a hoarder's den. Boxes and clothes and garbage kept Francine from even taking a step inside. They had to start by going through the unpacked boxes and putting things in their right place. They played music and danced and talked like before. Jenny felt much better with Francine around, though she refused to leave Francine's sight.

They had cleaned for nearly fourteen hours, but at last the entire house was done. Jenny could sleep in her own bed now, and it was made up with sheets and pillowcases and blankets. Francine was about to leave, but Jenny pleaded for her to just stay the night. Francine wouldn't have to work until later the next afternoon, and Jenny even offered the bed.

"No, that's okay," Francine assured. "The couch will be fine for me." Francine took the cushions off of the couch and folded it out into a bed. Jenny didn't want to admit that she didn't know it could do that.

Jenny and Francine fell asleep almost immediately. Their muscles ached and their eyes closed as soon as their heads hit their pillows. Francine curled up in the bed that folded out of the couch, sighing. She felt great for being able to help Jenny with the house. Francine hoped her friend would feel better now that the place was livable. She dreamed of images that didn't link together and would forget about most of it the next morning. However, later that night, she woke up for seemingly no cause. She checked her phone for the time. The blue clock flashed 3:21 PM. Francine groaned and turned her body, sure that it was because her side was beginning to ache.

She gasped and sat up instantly. Standing in front of the kitchen, sagging forward slightly, was a wrapped-up figure with black strands of hair sticking out of the head of the bandaged being. She grabbed her phone and directed light towards it.

The figure sagged even more, the bandages unwrapping from the body. Some of the flesh bandages slid off, the inside of the mummy was pitch black, and broke apart like clods of dirt, or like ash. It unwound, the black contents spilling on the carpet, the head of the being rolling to the floor. Francine screamed.

"Francine!"

Francine's eyes shot open, and had to close them again. The sun was too bright. She could make out Jenny's outline. "Jenny?" Her throat hurt for some reason.

"Francine you've been screaming in your sleep," Jenny cried. "Are you okay, what in the heck were you dreaming about?"

Francine scanned the living room, and after a moment her shoulders relaxed. "I don't remember," she lied.

GIRL ON THE BUS

Curt had always been a bus driver. Ever since he was a young man, he has driven the same route from downtown to the hill near the town's oldest High school and back. He was the driver of route 32. He knew all of the kids that went to the high school, he knew the families that lived on the roads he passed. A frail man in his fifties now, there were some frequent passengers that felt like family.

All of this was especially why he was so upset for being switched to route 26. It went from downtown to the valley and back. Being the longest route for the buses, Curt's usual route was given to a newer employee after the driver to route 26 passed away. Curt never liked the driver of that route. He was brash and short-tempered. His passing was something of a story to the bus crew, however. He was found alone at home with pictures of his late wife and daughter, and an autopsy was being done. The deceased driver seemed to have nothing wrong with his health. Some speculated a heart attack, others speculated poison or overdose.

Curt didn't care much for the cause, only the effect. Because of him, Curt had to leave his route and learn a new, longer one. Curt was always uneasy with change, so he had little hopes for this new route. It even passed the deceased driver's old home, an unpleasant reminder of why he was set in this position.

The weather was thankfully clear the first day of Curt's new drive on bus route 26. The second day, however, was pouring so hard that Curt was often delayed by reckless drivers speeding around him with limited vision. Not as many people got on the bus on that day, so this was the first time he noticed the little girl sitting farthest back. She couldn't have been older than twelve, but she was sitting quietly on the city bus by herself. Curt was curious at first, but he had to focus his attention on the unfamiliar road and so tried to pay the passengers little mind.

He drove all the way up to the valley, but still the girl had not left the bus. Curt didn't think much of it, as she seemed to be reading a book and maybe her stop was sometime on the way back, and just needed to get out of the rain to read. But as he drove all the way back downtown, the little girl still had not left her spot. Nobody paid her mind. No one had even looked her way.

Curt kept trying to ignore his curiosity. It wasn't his business what the little girl was doing or where she was going. It wasn't until the very last round of driving late that night that the young girl walked out of the bus at the last stop downtown.

The whole situation was strange to Curt. He had loiterers before, but never any so young as the little girl. She was so pale and so silent, and no one paid her any mind. It was almost as though she were a ghost. Ghosts, however, weren't real. There had to be a reason. Perhaps she was abused at home and was trying to stay away? She could be homeless, but child services would have found her by now, Curt thought. As he lay at home in his bed, he decided to gather the courage to speak to the little girl. He wasn't too sure why this passenger in particular caught his attention. He supposed because she seemed a little familiar. Still, he couldn't quite place it in his mind how he knew her.

He wasn't surprised to see her the next day. She entered the bus from the stop by the old driver's house, then sat in the back with a book in hand. He went about his route all the way down to the valley, and then he took his route back downtown. Once he got to the downtown station, he is allowed fifteen minutes of break to eat or relax while the bus gets filled with gas at the station. At this time, the girl was the only one on the bus. No one bothered to remove her.

After Curt finished his sandwich, gathering up the courage to confront her, he stood up from his seat and walked over to the girl. "Excuse me, miss."

The girl made no response.

"Miss?" Curt asked again. The girl still didn't move. Curt was beginning to lose his patience. Also, though he would never admit it, he was feeling afraid of the girl. "Miss can you hear me?"

"What?" The girl looked up from her book. Her eyes were a sad blue, almost forlorn. Curt felt sudden empathy, despite being unaware of the girl's situation. "Before we reach the valley, you'll have to get off the next time we pass your stop. You can't ride the bus the whole day."

The young woman's eyes widened. "But I have nowhere else to go," her voice breaking at the reply.

Curt made a sharp inhale. "You have family you can go home to, don't you?"

The young girl didn't respond.

"What's your name?" He asked.

The girl still did not respond, though she seemed in thought. "My name?" she repeated.

"Yes. You know your name, right?"

The girl kept mouthing the words 'my name,' her face scrunched and distressed. Curt could almost see through this girl. He was having a hallucination; he was losing it. His skin crawled as he watched this transparent young woman try desperately to remember her name. Curt's hand moved forward to touch her, he wanted to know if she was there. Would his hand go through her? Would she disappear?

"Don't touch me!" The girl screamed. Curt's hand reeled back and he looked at her, unaware that such a desperate shriek could come from such a small young woman. The two looked at each other in silence, Curt letting his irritation and fear get in the way of a clear head. If he ignored her maybe, then would she go away?

"Alright," he decided. He turned away hesitantly. Would she attack him? He sat at his seat and started the bus. She wasn't being violent; she wasn't even looking at him. He felt better after his first passengers got on, at least there were actual people in the bus now. After his first stop, he drove the path that ran beside the river which flowed through downtown. He looked down the cliff to the water for a brief moment, then his eye caught the rearview mirror, and with it the girl, ghost or hallucination, also looking out to the river.

That night, she exited the bus again at the last stop downtown. He had a thought to follow her, but not only was following a ghost in the middle of night absolutely not a good idea, but downtown was dangerous at this time. He got into his car to go home, but after watching the news and having dinner, he had a rough night of sleep. Who could he tell about this? Would anyone believe him? He tried to ask the other two drivers who take his route on the mornings and his days off if they remember a little girl who read at the back of the bus, and they both mentioned that the last few seats were always empty, even when the bus was otherwise crowded.

She came to the bus every single day. She always sat at the same place, and nobody bothered her. She read until the very last stop downtown where she would fade into the night towards the river glimmering in the distance. Curt had wanted to ask her questions, but ever since her outburst he never felt compelled enough to talk to her to actually do it.

Curt spent nearly seven months on that route, and not a day went by that he didn't see the young woman. He knew that she looked familiar, and tried to look around on his laptop and phone for pictures of people he knew, but he only had pictures of family, friends and coworkers. He once made a mistake of casually bringing up the girl on the bus who looked like someone he knew to his son, but Curt felt like he made his son too suspicious having no real reason or information besides how the girl looks, so he dropped the subject.

Midsummer, Curt noticed another young woman get on the bus and walk to the end. This woman was older than the girl in the back, but she sat next to the girl. Whether subconsciously avoiding the spirit or because they felt the same eerie skin-crawling sensation Curt did, no one before then ever sat at the back of the bus. The young woman's short black hair would often hide her face, but he saw her turn her head towards the little girl often.

With every stop, Curt watched this woman speak to the ghost. He waited to see when the girl would meet her stop. He noticed how the ghost girl never put her book down.

The woman stood up to leave at the downtown stop. Curt gripped her wrist and let go to get her attention. "Miss, will you wait one moment, I have a question to ask you."

The woman's violet eyes widened once she was confronted, but once she recognized she was in no trouble, or perhaps danger, she relaxed. "Sure, what do you want to ask me?"

Curt waited until everyone else had exited the bus. "Uh," he muttered. He closed the door. The woman's jaw tightened.

"Miss," Curt began. "By chance, do you see the girl sitting at the back of the bus?"

The woman looked behind her, relaxed, and turned back with a smile and a nod. "You can see her too."

"Yes," Curt's voice raised. "Yes, I do. Who is she? What's her name? Why is she here?"

"Oh, well," The woman's eyes trailed to the side. "Well, her name is Jill."

"Jill," Curt rested in his seat. Where had he heard that name?

"She doesn't seem to be able to remember much. It took a long time to remember her name. Her name is Jill, she said she was leaving. That's all I got."

"Leaving," Curt parroted. "Is she really a ghost? Have I gone crazy? I must have, I'm asking a young woman about a ghost as though you would have all the answers." It occurred to him how strange this situation was.

"Well, I can see her too, so you're probably just relieved that you're not the only one. That happens to me a lot."

"You're saying that you see a lot of them?"

"Yeah," The woman replied. "I see them all the time. Others see them sometimes though, I believe, if they're meant to help the spirit."

"Help her," Curt furrowed his brow. "I just want this to be over." He wanted his old route still, more than anything.

"She does too, I bet," The woman looked back at the girl reading the book.

Curt moved his head to the side, his eyes set on this strange woman. "Who are you, miss?"

"Hm?" The woman turned to look at Curt. "Oh, I'm Geraldine. What's your name?"

"Curt," he replied skeptically. "You know about these ghosts, you say. What am I supposed to do about her?"

"Well," Geraldine shrugged. "You might need to help her move on."

"How? Why me?"

Geraldine shrugged again, "It's different depending on what happened to her. Curt, sir, how come that after you realized Jill was a ghost, you didn't demand a different bus route, or change jobs altogether? Most people would have run screaming."

"What?" Curt thought it was a stupid question at first, but while he thought about what most others would have done, he realized the idea of leaving the route because of the ghost didn't once occur to him.

"Anyway," Geraldine sighed. "I have to go meet up with a friend. Good luck, Curt."

Curt realized that Geraldine was waiting for him to let her out. He opened the door. "But what am I supposed to do?"

"Beats me," Geraldine replied.

That night, when the last stop was made, the little girl got up and left the bus again and faded into the dark city. Curt went home, watched the news, and went to bed. He was unable to sleep, he looked at his ceiling with bloodshot eyes. Questions and confused thoughts rattled in his brain. He tried to remember where he heard the name 'Jill.' He knew he met the little girl before.

He thought again about why. Why didn't he run away? He had no doubt that he was afraid of the ghost. However, after a while of thinking he realized that, while he was afraid of the ghost, he was sorry for the girl. Something had happened to her. She was alone in a bus. He thought of what the girl said to him, and he thought of what Geraldine said to him. The girl was running away, that much was clear. He met her before, when she was alive, which was also clear. The nagging feeling of recognition which he would usually ignore mixed with the knowledge of some terrible occurrence which led this girl to haunt this bus route led Curt with a feeling of curiosity mixed with dread. Could he have done something? Is her death his fault somehow? Why else would he be the only one to see her?

Curt spent his morning going through his photos again. He thought of all the people he could remember from his old route. He thought about people he may have spoken to. After a few moments of looking through, he came across a bundle of pictures from a business party. His heart skipped a beat. Something clicked in his mind. With a weak, shaky grip, he pulled the photos out. A few years ago, the bus service had a party at the station to celebrate the company's hundred years. Curt was the only one who didn't bring family members along. They had the party at the downtown station.

Jill always arrived on the bus at the stop near the house of the driver that passed away. The driver had a wife at one point before she left, and he also had a daughter at one point that went missing.

Jillian Gulliver, daughter to Daniel Gulliver. She had long blond hair and sad, almost frightened eyes.

Curt dropped the photos to the ground, some falling into the picture box while others spilled to the side of it. A picture of Curt chatting with some friends remained in his mind where there sat a sad little girl sitting alone by the snack table. Curt covered his mouth. There was no doubt about it.

Curt was distracted throughout the whole day at work. He drove the route mechanically, unable to face the little girl sitting alone in the back. He couldn't eat during his breaks. Near the end of the day, Curt looked back to the girl who sat alone reading her book. His throat was dry, his body weak with fatigue and hunger. "Jillian Gulliver," he whispered, but got no response. He didn't speak loud enough. "Jillian Gulliver," Curt repeated. The little girl looked up at him.

Jill and Curt kept their gaze on each other for what felt like an eternity, an empty aisle was all that kept them apart. The more Curt looked at her the hollower the eyes seemed to become. Curt was transfixed in horror and unease as he watched her image fade from a young child to a rotting corpse. Her eyes faded in and out of view, leaving the sockets behind. Her skin bloated and rotted away, her mouth opened to rotting teeth and black bile seeping from out her throat.

Curt looked away, sick to his stomach. When he looked back Jillian was reading her book like normal.

The final stop arrived that night. Jillian stood from her seat and glided out of the bus. Curt turned the ignition off. She made no sign of noticing him following her. Downtown was dangerous at night, but Curt's curiosity and guilt was like a poison which promised to consume him if he didn't answer her silent cries. Jillian walked past homeless men and shady alleyway lurkers. Curt made no eye contact and prayed he would not become another ghost to go down this path. Curt followed the girl to the bridge over the large river. Jillian stopped. She turned her head towards the edge of the bridge. Curt saw her tear-stained face. Jillian leaned over. She leaned more. Her cries were drowned by the rapids below. The book fell from her hand. She was about to fall.

"Wait," Curt called to her. He couldn't even hear himself say it. He made no motion to stop her or to catch her. There was no reason to, it had already been done.

Her body disappeared in the roaring river. Curt went to where she had been standing moments before. Years before. His eyes scanned the black water for any sign of her. He went to the other side of the bridge to look downriver. He went down the cold steel stairs to the bank and walked along it, ignoring the confetti of trash underneath the bridge. Did anyone see her? Did anyone care?

It was too dark to see any further, the streetlamps didn't go this far. Curt pulled out his cell phone to use what little light it could emit to push on. Several times he became afraid and thought about turning back, but the image of the little girl and a sharp stab of regret pressed him further, until…

There was a news report the following day. Local bus driver finds the body of Jillian Gulliver, a twelve-year-old that went missing three years ago. Curt sat at home late that night watching the news. An old, water-damaged copy of short stories lay on his coffee-table. Curt turned off the television and went to bed early that night.

When he was given the option to go back to his old route weeks later, he politely declined. After so many months, he had gotten used to his longer route. Still, it was a little strange to see people sitting in the back seat. He would have to get used to that.

IT WASN'T A BEAR

There are many people who do not believe, or care about, the idea of spirits or demons existing in the world with us. Truly, the only people who seem to believe in the existence of such beings are the ones that had experienced them firsthand. For Paulina, however, these beings are undeniably and inexplicably real.

She sat around with a group of friends one afternoon, enjoying a board game and eventually taking part in conversations so engaging they all forgot whose turn was next and stopped playing the game altogether. Paulina drank a cherry sports drink while she listened to the other three girls in attendance marvel at the idea of ghosts, Elena having brought it up. She claims she had seen, for a brief moment, a chair in her house move on its own. Linda was enamored by the tale, but Rosaline was not convinced. Rosaline had a bachelor's degree in physics, and had a very strict realistic mind. Linda did not believe in such things either, but liked to fantasize the idea anyway. She was fond of daydreaming, and such stories, or illusions as she saw them, gave her enough daydream fuel to last her for days. Paulina was very silent, listening to Elena as she recalled the event.

"It was last week, or actually, I think it was two weeks ago. Yes, two weeks, because it was before I bought the new shutters for the kitchen windows. I was trying to fix the old shutters in the kitchen at the time, since the cat got herself stuck in them again. The new ones are wooden shutters so I'm hoping that it will be less enticing for Meowdusa to get caught in. Rosaline you really should bring Tank over for another kitty playdate, she's getting really rowdy without her friend around. Anyway, yes, I was fixing the shutters. I heard a squeak. Well not a squeak more like a 'rrrrt,' you know, like chairs being moved on hardwood floor. I thought it was Meowdusa at first but I looked at her and she was asleep on her kitty playground in the hole at the top, you know, the place where she likes to sleep because the sun hits that spot? Anyway, I knew it wasn't her. I got curious with finding out where the noise came from. It was in the dining room, and I thought maybe my husband had come home but he wouldn't be back until later that night. He was at the pub with the boys, Paulina, you know, with your fiancée and with the guys at work. So no, it wasn't him."

"I love you Elena," Linda interrupted. "But can we have less backstory?"

"You saw a chair move on your own, the end," Rosaline confirmed.

"Really, you two are too cruel. It's not the destination, it's the trip. I'm providing atmosphere."

"You're right, sorry. Go on," Linda sighed.

"Anyway," Elena thought for a bit to remember her place. "It wasn't Rolf. I was a little spooked. I took a wooden spoon with me, it was all I had within reach, and I went into the dining room. The second I looked towards the table; I saw it. 'rrrrt,' went the chair, and it scooted itself back in, right where it was before."

"You were hearing things," Rosaline sighed. "When a person is home alone it's easy for them to fall for mind tricks like that."

"No, I don't think it was a trick. It was too real; I saw it move. It moved and nothing was even close to it."

Linda thought a moment. "Imagine it though, your house haunted. What a considerate ghost to scoot his chair in when he was done with it."

"There aren't any ghosts," Rosaline stated. "From where your kitchen is and that dining room table, you would have been too far to know for sure. Perhaps your cat had a gastrointestinal issue and that's what made the noise, which spooked you."

"No, I'm sure it was the chair. You don't believe me?"

"It could have been a ghost," Paulina spoke up. "It isn't impossible."

"It is impossible, because they don't exist," Rosaline stated again.

"Imagine if they did though, it would be quite interesting, wouldn't it? Imagine a spectral house-guest. Do you suppose they would want to eat something 'light?'"

"Linda that was a horrible joke. And yes," Paulina laughed. "I have seen a spirit, and there is no doubt about it. That is how I know they exist." Pauline moved forward on the couch. Rosaline stayed comfortably sunk into the lazy-chair, but the other two girls were perplexed at Paulina's addition to the conversation. The three women looked over to her and listened.

"George and I live in the woods, in the middle of nowhere. As you girls know. We get bears trying to come into the house or eat our rabbits every so often. There are a lot of strange noises that happen at night, but my fiancée and I know we're safe because if it were a bear or something else trying to harm our rabbits, our dog Nora would raise a fuss. We've grown accustomed to the sound of rustling leaves and animal sounds around the house. In the fall, nearing winter is when the bears and coyotes are at their worse because it's so close to the time when food will be scarce. I keep my senses heightened at this time of year for Nora's barking so I can chase away the predators."

"One night, there was no sound of rustling. Yet Nora started to growl. It took me a moment to wake up, it was nearly two in the morning. I still hadn't heard anything, but Nora's growling insisted there was something outside. Instead of going back to bed, I became curious and woke myself up, got my slippers and a coat, and wandered outside to see what might be going on. Nora was acting strangely, staying close to my side instead of chasing whatever bear or coyote was spooking her. She kept looking out into the forest, but there was nothing there."

Paulina took another gulp of her drink. "I was concerned, to be honest. Nora had never acted like that. So I decided that I would walk into the forest to see what it was that spooked her. If I could find the culprit, then I would know what it is that made Nora react as she was and know how to handle it. The lack of sound also unnerved me. Aside from my own breathing and Nora's growling, the woods were unsettlingly silent. I could hear a leaf fall. So I took a flashlight and one of George's plastic guns that shot the Styrofoam bullets, which would do no damage but was loud enough to startle a bear, and walked into the woods towards the direction Nora was growling."

The girls noticed, as Paulina's voice lowered to a more haunting tone, that the sky was darker than they remembered. It had crept up on them, and the tree branches of Lidia's living room window cast an outstretched shadow over them, as though the woods had followed Paulina from her little trailer out in the middle of nowhere. Despite being in the comfort of a small house, they felt the chill of the forest and even Rosaline bent forward to listen to Paulina's story.

"The air was chilly that night, though not even the wind had dared make a sound. Nora's growling and our footsteps were all I could hear, as though we were truly alone in the woods. We had wandered just out of sight from the trailer when I noticed movement. I thought it was a shadow at first with the way it disappeared. I kept my flashlight low, but after a time Nora would no longer follow with me. She stood still, nose pointed to the direction of the shadow, and growled. I patted my leg, told her to come, 'Aqui,' I called. But she only looked up at me before turning back to the fading sight of the shadow, growling again."

"It was perhaps the size of a black bear from what I could tell with my limited vision. I walked closer to it as it wandered further into the trees. The air gave me a chill, but I kept a tight hold onto my flashlight. I dared to illuminate more of the beast from behind."

"It had no fur. It had no paws. It looked like a tree trunk, but it bent and moved and swirled like shadows. I thought it might have been a hallucination, but I was following it, and it never faded from my sight. I could only see the leg. I panicked, admittedly. I had seen nothing like it, I became almost desperate to see the entire creature. I wanted to be sure I wasn't hallucinating or dreaming. It moved irregularly, almost somber, or as though it wasn't sure the next step would be into solid ground."

"Did you see its face?" Elena whispered. Paulina nodded, "Yes. But not until later. After I got over my surprise, and was more curious than anything, I started to follow the beast. Its legs moved a body that was completely hidden among the tree branches, its steps making no sound, never turning to me once."

Paulina took a second of silence to have a drink. All three of Paulina's friends seemed interested including the skeptical Rosaline. "I noticed after a while that I had lost track of where I was. Nora wasn't with me anymore, and I was following a strange creature deeper into the woods. I had thought we would have hit another house by the time I thought of it, but it was still nothing except woods as far as I could tell. I had no sense of direction. Then I saw more of them."

Linda gasped, "More than one of them?" Paulina nodded in response. "I noticed one from the corner of my eye, and about five or six more started to roam into a clearing. It was then that I saw their faces." Paulina closed her eyes and envisioned it, giving a light shudder. "It wasn't a black fog like the rest of it. It was as if it was wearing a mask; a white mask with irregularly shaped eyes and a mouth agape. The neck was long and crooked and jagged. The neck itself, I imagine, could have been six feet long."

Paulina opened her eyes and looked right at her friend's faces.

"They paid no mind to me, until one of them who turned its mask my way. It froze, and so did I. More of them turned toward me and froze, like statues."

Linda and Elena's breaths sharpened in protest at the same time. "They stared at me, frozen, fading in and out except for their faces, which remained white and staring and none of us dared make a movement. All of them were looking at me now, staring. They were frozen, unnaturally. I'm not sure, but they seemed more still than any living thing could be. They were perfectly still until I shifted my weight."

"All at once, their mask-like faces started shuddering. They started a rattling sound, and they were getting louder and louder. Their wide-open mouths seemed to cry out in horrified agony. Their heads and necks darted and shivered as the rattling became louder and louder. The first one that noticed me moved closer to me. I wanted to run, but I was paralyzed with fear."

"The rattling was getting so loud I couldn't hear anything else. Especially since before, everything was quiet, the sight of them and the loud rattling almost caused me to faint. But then, the rattling changed into screaming, the sort of scream I imagined their wide eyes and mouth to make." Paulina wrapped her arms around each other. "I turned and I ran. Like a sudden push into reality, I heard leaves rustling again, and the wind was howling as though making up for its silence moments before. It couldn't, however, drown out the shrieking."

I ran and ran; my legs were scratched by the twigs under me. I didn't know where I was, and I thought I was being followed. I heard rustling behind me. Something was gaining on me. I burst through another clearing and there it was: my trailer. But I kept running, the rustling behind me was coming faster. I cried out in terror, and it was Nora that burst out of the forest. She ran past me and to the door of the trailer."

"I looked back into the woods. Nora waited for me at the door of the trailer, and I no longer heard any rattling or screeching. However, I did hear the wind. Soon, I heard the owls and the opossums moving around as well. I hurried back inside with Nora and I couldn't sleep the rest of the night until George came home that morning."

"Did you tell him the story?" Linda asked.

Paulina shook her head. "I've only told you girls." Paulina

looked over to Rosaline who had been attentively listening to the story. She could tell that Rosaline was trying to explain the phenomenon in her mind. Paulina turned her body towards her dear friend. "I was wide awake in the middle of the night and didn't imagine anything I saw. I don't know what you think it might have been: an illusion, a mistake, maybe I made it up. But I still have the scratches on my ankle from the bushes I ran through and my pajama bottoms are torn. I ran away from something that night, and it was no bear."

THE MOSQUITO QUEEN

> Blood drips from her pores,
> An insect is made,
> When in sight there's cause to be afraid,
> She'll make your eyes bleed,
> Sight never unseen,
> They all hail to The Mosquito Queen

Delilah couldn't remember where she first heard the poem, but she was always unnerved by it. Perhaps she read it first on the internet somewhere, but no, she had the strangest memory of seeing the poem in print first somewhere. Regardless, it gave her chills.

She normally didn't like spooky stuff and it wasn't something she liked to think of often, but for some reason at seemingly random times the poem would come back to her like a haunting melody. This time was one of those times, as she ran on the treadmill in the 'Bronze Biceps' Gym. She noted how the sweat was getting into her eyes and making them sting, which what brought her mind to 'make your eyes bleed.'

She stopped running on the treadmill to hit the showers so she could wash away the sweat. Cooling down in the pool might be nice after the shower, she thought. She had to be somewhere close to the dumbbells so that when her boyfriend and training partner Jerry arrived, they could meet up. The dumbbells area faced the window-wall that led to the pool, so it would be easy to catch him once he came in. After the shower and she got dressed, she found a spot on the pool where she could swim idly and relax. It felt so nice to have a place to cool down after such rigorous running. She could feel her muscles relax in the fresh, cool water as it lifted her from the floor and carried her with its small current caused by the lot of twelve-year-olds on the other corner of the pool splashing each other. Delilah herself was not too fond of kids. If they didn't come bother her, she didn't mind them, but other times she had little patience for kids that would come and bug her. 'An insect is made.'

She had become nice and relaxed after ten minutes into the pool when she noted that Jerry was still not around. He was already almost an hour late at this point and it concerned her. Delilah hopped out of the pool to dry herself off, and she went to grab her cell phone.

Delilah crossed one arm over her body and propped her other elbow on the wrist, her cheek leaning into the receiver.

A loud ringing came from her other ear, and it made her heart nearly jump out of her mouth. She screamed and dropped her phone, turning around to hit her boyfriend's chest with her fist.

"Haha, owwwwwch that hurt, Lilah."

"Don't you dare sneak up on me like that, what the heck is wrong with you?!" She pouted through clenched teeth, picking up her phone to make sure it wasn't broken.

"I'm sorry," Jerry laughed. "When I didn't see you at the dumbbells, I thought you'd be at the treadmill but when I didn't see you I went to the showers to get ready and on my way out here you were. I knew you were calling me and I couldn't resist."

"Why were you late?" She demanded. "I waited for like an hour."

"There was some sort of accident on the highway. I waited in that traffic jam for like 45 minutes. I tried to text you to say I was going to be late; didn't you get the text?"

"No, I didn't get any text," Delilah grumbled. She looked at her phone and saw '1 new message.' "Yes, I got the text."

"Well it's cool, I'm here now. You still want me to school you- I mean, spot you on the weights?"

Delilah smirked a little. Their little rivalries were what got them motivated to work out. It was so much better doing that sort of thing together rather than being alone. "So, you think you can outweigh me, thunder-thighs?"

"Whoah, who's calling who thunder-thighs? I don't think I appreciate that sort of bullying I should report you to the gym staff." The two wandered into the weight room. Delilah and Jerry exchanged witty banter between each other as they stretched their muscles.

"Oh, that's right I forgot, you're soooo sensitive," Delilah mocked.

"At least I'm not so easily startled by the littlest things like the sound of a ringing cellphone."

"You want to know something, Wyler?"

"Oh, so we're going by last names now, Miss O'Donahue?"

"How about we let our muscles do the talking? I have a good idea how it's going to end- with me kicking your butt."

"Oh but 'tis I, fair lady, who will be the kicker on yonder ass."

"Okay nerd, how about you spot me and we'll see whom shall kickest which ass."

Jerry followed Delilah to the weight bench. The goal was to bench press ten more than the most weight the other person could. Jerry surpassed Delilah with upper body weight, but Delilah was far ahead in leg weights. She could run much faster, though Jerry was more flexible. They were nearly the exact same when swimming, which was the last thing they did. To wind down before going home, the two of them went into the sauna together.

"I love how they make this room smell like peppermint, it's so refreshing," Delilah sighed.

"It's definitely better than the smell of sweat," Jerry agreed. He took off his glasses and set them to the side, more tired with trying to keep them from getting fogged up than he was about not being able to see anything.

'Blood drips from her pores.'

"Hey, Jerry?"

"Hm?"

"You know the scary story with that mosquito lady? Do you know where the poem for her originated?"

"I'unno, why are you asking?"

"It's just been in my head all day, and it creeps me out. I thought if I knew where it came from, I don't know, maybe it won't seem as scary."

"Lilah, the Mosquito Queen is just a myth, don't worry about it, okay?"

"You can't just tell me not to worry about it, when has that ever worked for anyone?"

Jerry sighed. "I'll look it up at some point when I'm at work, okay? Are we still on for dinner tomorrow?"

"You bet, thank you," Delilah smiled. Jerry was great at finding out almost anything. He was a big nerdy know-it-all and Delilah loved him for it. She knew that if anyone could rifle through all the phony original content and get to the real truth, it would be Jerry. He had plenty of time working at the library. Not many people really went to the public library anymore so he had more time than Delilah, who worked retail at an appliance store. Her knowledge was extensive in how to fix vacuums, refrigerators and microwaves. She knew what brands were better than others and how to best rig up computers and televisions. She didn't have much patience trying to research stuff like Jerry did. Jerry was book-smart, and Delilah felt no shame in admitting her silly boyfriend's greatest strength.

The end of the day came crashing onto the earth, and Delilah was exhausted. She got home and immediately plopped down with leftover pizza and a beer. As she enjoyed a game show, she heard a buzzing. It made her jump, and she almost dropped her beer. In the apartment, a mosquito was flying around.

Jenny felt her spine freeze. She wanted to kill it, but she didn't want to kill it. It sounded stupid, but she didn't want to incur the wrath of the Mosquito Queen should she exist. Delilah found a cup in the kitchen, hunted the mosquito down and put the cup over it before it was able to fly away. "A-ha! Caught you. Now I can decide what to do with you tomorrow…"

She wouldn't get the opportunity to do anything to it the next morning. She walked over to the glass and the mosquito had disappeared. "What," she could have sworn that she trapped it. She hoped it didn't bite her overnight. She felt herself getting itchy just from the idea, and hurried to get ready for the day.

She was especially looking forward to dinner later that night. She waited in front of the barbecue restaurant while wearing a flowing blue sundress with butterfly patterns and a matching satchel purse. She blushed, not being used to wearing anything so flattery, but she wanted to feel especially fancy for the dinner and had a slight excitement in sur Prining Jerry whenever she had the chance. 'Wow, I didn't recognize you,' she expected him to say. Or maybe just a stunned look of admiration. Of course, knowing him, he wouldn't even say anything about it. There was that possibility. Though to be honest, she would prefer anything but that. She went to a lot of trouble to look nice. She even wore the heirloom flower clip her mother gave her to pull back her hair, which exploded into curls of ebony underneath.

Delilah noticed Jerry's car pulling into the driveway moments before their intended meet time. Jerry always cut his time close, she thought with a sigh. Her stomach was growling, and had lost passion in keeping her posture. She watched him park and walk out of the car with a t-shirt and a worn pair of jeans. She smiled at him as he walked up to her.

"You look nice," he kissed her cheek. "Aren't you cold though?"

'You look nice.' It wasn't poetry, but he did notice. It was more than she hoped to expect, and it made her heart flutter all the same. "No, I'm not cold. How was work?"

"I researched that poem you wanted me to, and I have some interesting news to tell you."

"Yeah?" Delilah's stomach lurched at remembering what she asked him.

"Let's go ahead and have a seat first though. I'm so hungry I could eat everything on the menu."

They were seated for two overlooking the garden park across the street. The sun was setting, and they sat there together waiting for their orders to arrive. Delilah's attention had turned towards the poem again. She wasn't certain why it had started to bother her, but she somehow felt as though it was something important to her. It was a code that needed unlocking, or a story without an end.

"Okay, you wanted to know about the poem about the Mosquito Queen, so I did a little digging online. As far as I can tell, it doesn't go very far back. It seems as though the poem started with someone online inside of a scary story webpage."

"Oh, so it's just a story," Delilah relaxed.

"Not exactly."

Delilah's eyes darted to his to see if he was joking, or trying to scare her. "What do you mean by 'not exactly?'"

"I said the 'poem' started out online. The Mosquito Queen story goes back much, much farther. The story itself has only been written recently, in one or two books. The oral tradition goes back to a small band of tribesman hundreds of years ago. It's only now gained recognition from the poem."

"So, what you're telling me is the Mosquito Queen is a real thing?"

Jerry laughed. "What? Lilah, it's just a ghost story. It's old, sure, but it was probably just a cautionary story. The Mosquito Queen was a forest spirit that was cut down and deformed by a man who eventually paid the price. Sometimes he was just blinded, sometimes he was turned into a mosquito, sometimes he was sucked dry of all his blood, it depends on where you heard the story. The tribesmen probably just made the story to warn people about forgetting the spirits or not being kind to nature or something like that. That's all it is."

Delilah knew she should have felt better with what he said, but she couldn't bring herself to. She only kept thinking about the mosquito that went missing in her room. They ate together and had conversation that had Delilah forget about it. She didn't think of the Mosquito Queen again until it was time for them to part ways. The sky was black now, and darker with the clouds hiding the stars and moon. "Jerry," Delilah called out.

Jerry looked at her and smiled, "Yeah?"

"Could I maybe spend the night with you tonight?"

"Oh? Oh!"

"Not like that."

"Oh. Sure Delilah, is something wrong?"

"I'm just a little spooked, that's all," she admitted. Delilah held her arms over her chest. It was colder tonight than she thought it would be.

"Awww," Jerry sighed, but dared not say any more. "Sure, drive on over. The place isn't that clean, though."

"That's alright," Delilah replied. She got used to his sloppiness by now, and he wasn't all that bad to begin with. She drove her car behind his and they both parked over at the duplex he lived in. The other half of the house was for sale. Delilah joked sometimes about buying the other half but they weren't ready for that sort of step. For the time being, Jerry just had half of the house.

They went in together, talking about work and their family. Delilah mused that she hadn't seen her family in a while, while Jerry's parents call him almost every day. Jerry offered to sleep on the couch while she took the bed, but Delilah didn't want to be far from Jerry, so they decided to sleep in the bed together.

Jerry went into his bedroom to grab some clothes Delilah left at his house earlier, and to also get her a big shirt and boxers to sleep in. As the couple got ready for bed, Delilah heard a buzzing.

"What's that," she cried. She looked around her until she met Jerry's eye contact.

"What's what?" Jerry asked. He caught sight of something flying around. "Oh, stupid mosquitoes."

"Wait Jerry, don't-," Delilah tried to stop Jerry before he tried to kill the mosquito, but Jerry had already slammed a book on top of the insect which landed on the desk. Delilah felt her stomach sink. "Jerry, what have you done?"

"What, you wanted to save the insect? It would just bite us overnight, I'd rather not go to work scratching all day, wouldn't you?"

"But the Mosquito Queen," Delilah sounded desperate now, wishing for Jerry to understand.

"You're still on about that story? Lilah, my dearest butterbean," Jerry put his hands on both of Delilah's cheeks, squishing her face a little. "There is no such thing as a Mosquito Queen. Well, perhaps there's a queen mosquito in bug terminology I don't really know, but there is no evil deformed spirit sucking people dry of their blood. Even if there was, I would beat it up."

Delilah laughed through her squished cheeks. "You're going to beat up a deadly spirit?"

"I'd beat up a hundred if it made you feel better," Jerry grinned.

After a few moments, the two went to sleep. They cuddled together beneath the thin sheets and blanket with Delilah's head resting at the crook of Jerry's neck. They were intertwined, they were calm and they were satisfied.

Delilah heard buzzing.

Delilah was so tired, and it was hard to force her sleepy mind away from the dream she was having. Jerry was snoring loudly, but the buzzing wasn't coming from him.

"Jerry," She whispered. She nudged him, but he didn't stir. Delilah peeked through his arm into the darkness. It didn't sound like an insect. It was building up to almost a swarm of them. Delilah's breathing quickened, nudging Jerry harder. "Jerry, wake up, the insects, wake up," she hissed.

"Mmh, huh, what?" Jerry mumbled. Delilah was silent for a few seconds as Jerry turned his head around a moment. "What's that noise?" Jerry turned to flip on his desk lamp.

The light was turned on, but even then, it was dim with a number of mosquitoes crawling on the lightbulb. Delilah and Jerry both jumped up in bed, looking around in horror. The room was swarming with the little insects. Jerry's closet door slowly started to open.

"Nope," Jerry cried before grabbing Delilah's hand and running out of his room. He slammed the door behind them, but as he went to open the door the handle was swarming with insects. Jerry swallowed his disgust to grab the handle, but not only would the handle not budge, the mosquitoes on the doorknob flew to cover

Jerry's hand and wrist before he hollered and frantically tried to wipe the mosquitoes away from him. "Ew ew ew!"

"Jerry, what's happening," Delilah cried, looking back at the bedroom, watching with terror as the door slowly started to open.

Jerry kicked the door, but only splintered it. "Delilah, help me out here!"

Delilah kicked the door and managed to bust a hole through to freedom. The impact hurt Delilah's leg, and the wood splinters cut into her skin, but her fear numbed the pain. Jerry tore himself through the door first, making way for Delilah to follow.

As soon as the two of them made it outside, they both stopped and held each other closer. There was the profile of a woman, crouched and nude, her body curved and her hair ratted and falling over her face. In the dim light they could only notice the back and spine lit by the moon, but she was bleeding. The blood didn't come from any cut, but it seemed to sweat out of her before the droplets of blood would disappear. She was swarmed by mosquitoes, and slowly, her head started to turn toward them.

"Don't look, just run!" Jerry shouted to Delilah. Both of them shouted for help in the little suburban area, but all the houses were instead dark and swarming with mosquitoes. Nobody came to help them, and with every place they tried to run, the Mosquito Queen crouched there, waiting. Delilah and Jerry both shut their eyes at the sight of her.

Delilah thought how stupid they were for not grabbing their car keys. If they could drive fast enough, then maybe they could survive.

Suddenly, Jerry stopped running.

"This is stupid. We can't run from it," Jerry turned his gaze to Delilah, his jaw trembling. "We might as well fight."

"Are you crazy?!" Delilah hit his shoulder in hopes of whacking sense into him. "You can't beat up a spirit Jerry what the heck are you thinking?!"

"Well running and shouting is getting us nowhere, so the last thing to do is punch that stupid spirit in her stupid face! Delilah, go hide somewhere."

"You're an idiot, Jerry! I'm telling you, if you try to punch her you're going to die!"

"That's why I'm telling you to hide, Delilah," Jerry turned his gaze to her. She felt his hand trembling in hers, she had never seen him so scared, but he spoke as evenly and convincing as he could. "It'll be fine. Just let me do this."

Delilah didn't know what he was trying to say. Did the running get the best of him? Did he think this was a dream? Delilah was scared, and the cut on her leg was starting to hurt. She limped behind a neighbor's fence and watched through the cracks.

"Come on, then! Come at me!" Jerry cried out, his voice and legs shaking. Delilah grit her teeth.

The swarming sound came closer and closer. Jerry stood in the middle of the street, waiting for the Mosquito Queen to come over to him. Delilah watched in horror as Jerry turned and there she was, staring at him.

Jerry was caught off-guard for a second, but closed his eyes and, waiting for something horrible to happen, ran at her with his fist rushing toward her.

He didn't feel anything contact his hand. He opened his eyes to see what happened.

His eyes went to his fist. It was swarming with mosquitoes. It was stuck in place. Jerry tried to retrieve his hand. He didn't want to look at her. The punch seemed to go through her chest, or rather, her body parted from the fist and now the mosquitoes are there, biting his arm, swarming out of the terrible woman and onto the rest of his body. He tried to punch with his other hand, but the swarm was all over him now, tickling his flesh. He screamed.

Delilah tried to stand up, but she was petrified. She watched the image of the Mosquito Queen become a swarm, and as they consumed Jerry his screams became faint, and he started to sway. 'They're sucking him dry!' She thought. Finding the strength to stand at last, she turns to go around the fence. 'I have to save Jerry,' was all she could think.

Once she had turned the corner of the fence, standing before her was the Mosquito Queen. She grinned an unnatural grin, her black hair fell around her, her eyes black as void had only two small white pupils staring right into Delilah's eyes. Delilah gasped, but she was too paralyzed. She couldn't close her eyes. She couldn't even move her head. She felt something hot fall down her cheeks. Tears? No… Blood.

Her vision blurred and filled with red. She screamed in agony. She begged for someone. She begged for Jerry. Everything went dark.

The following morning, no witness could recall hearing any foul play. Some people who had even been awake at the time claim that everything was peaceful all night. However, when the neighborhood woke up, the duplex door was splintered open. There was a dead man in the middle of the street, his body withered and sucked clean, covered in small red dots where his pores were as though he bled out of them himself. A woman could be heard crying hysterically, blood dried down her eyes. She called for Jerry. But she never saw him, or anything else, again.

BY THE RIVERSIDE

By the riverside there were houses, their backyards sharing the bank of the snaking body of water. It wound around for thirteen miles, starting from up the mountain and down a waterfall to the town below and ended with the lake in the valley. By the riverside, many children played in their backyards. They splashed their feet and legs into the cool water or taught their toys how to swim.

By the riverside, a body was found. She had only been dead for a few hours, but she had also been alive for only a few years. Five years old, her body was taken to the hospital. Her parents mourned and so did the rest of the town. Ever since, towns took extra precaution to keep children from playing in the water.

By the riverside, ten years later, a young boy and his family moved into a house for sale. They were warned from letting the boy play in the river, but the parents who had never suffered the loss of a child did not see any harm in it. The boy's favorite thing to do in the water was to splash with his toys. He noticed how no children lived in the neighboring houses, and the six-year-old boy would often get lonely. He found comfort in the water, however, and liked how nice and cool it was. He liked watching the minnows swim and kiss his toes when he stood still.

As the weather got colder, he still liked to watch the water glisten in the sunlight. He tossed pebbles into the water, or he would put leaves in the water and watch them float away. His parents found delight in knowing their son loved being outside so much, and were concerned only with hearing the story of the drowned girl. 'But it was ten years ago,' the father would remind the mother. The mother agreed, nodding her head, but would still often look outside just in case.

One day, during the first truly cold day of autumn, the boy ran inside excitedly, drenched and beaming. "Mommy," he cried. "I made a friend by the river!"

His mother and father looked at each other, but his mother hadn't seen him with anyone all day. She assumed he meant that it was someone like an imaginary friend. "Oh really," she asked. "What's his name?"

"It's a girl, mommy," the boy put his hands on his hips. "And she doesn't have a name. I call her 'river girl,'" which he claimed with a beaming smile.

"River Girl, hm?" The father exchanged glances with the mother. He seemed wary about this imaginary friend. "What does she look like?"

"She's smaller than me, with long yellow hair. She has big eyes and she says she loves to splash like I do!"

Their son was so happy to have made a friend, so though they were curious about their son having never had an imaginary friend before now, they had dinner with their son without speaking again about the river girl.

The boy went out the next day after school to the river holding a plastic triceratops. He hurried to the water and called out 'River Girl,' expecting someone to arrive to him. His mother watched as he looked upstream, smiled and said 'there you are.' But there was no one there. She left her son to play while she prepared for work, having to leave immediately after her husband came home from his job.

Later that night the boy's father told his son to come in and bring his toys.

"I let the River Girl borrow them," The boy replied.

"What, that's ridiculous. Bring them inside before they get ruined."

The boy said again that he didn't have his toys. When the father went to the back to find them himself, he noticed that there were no toys in the back yard at all. It was too dark to see in the river, but he was sure his son wouldn't throw all of his toys down there. He was very fond of the triceratops toy. The father decided that his son must have brought them inside before and was hiding in his room somewhere. The two ate dinner, and the son went to bed while the father stayed up to wait for his wife to come home from work.

This would happen for the next week. The boy would bring a toy outside, but not have it when he came in. His mother spent a few hours walking downstream, trying to see if she could find the toys in there. With no luck, she came back home and shared her baffled reaction with her husband. Her husband spent hours cleaning his room, but the toys that had gone missing never showed up. They told their son he wasn't allowed to bring toys to the river anymore, and he cried and screamed. Eventually, he calmed down, and he didn't send more toys to the river.

One morning, the mother heard something from the boy that gave her chills up her spine. "The River Girl wants me to go visit her house," he told her. "Can I go?"

Her fear made it through her voice. "What?! No you can't go to her house. You cannot ever leave the back yard do you hear me?"

The boy was shocked to tears with his mother's reaction. "But," he began. "She says she comes to my house all the time and I never come to hers."

"Well," the mother replied, thinking quickly. "If her parents allow her to come and visit you then okay. But your father and I, as your parents, are telling you no."

"She doesn't even tell her parents she's leaving. She just does," The boy muttered.

"Well that's-," the mother had to be careful not to raise her voice again. "That's something she'll have to talk with her parents about. But as for your father and I, if we see you not in the back yard and you go to see your friend's house without our permission, then you are going to be in a lot of trouble."

That seemed to end the conversation, but it had his mother watching the back yard twice as much as before.

It would become a relief when winter arrived, they thought. The water would be too cold for their son to play in and they could keep him indoors where it was safe. However, they didn't count on him sitting at the river bank, tossing rocks and talking to himself once the water got too cold to jump in. The parents decided it was for the best for them to take their son to a psychiatrist. It could be that he wasn't making friends in school, or that he was being bullied, or that he didn't like his classes. They wanted anything to turn up, anything that could be fixed.

They arranged for the boy to meet up with a counselor twice a week, and on those two days, for an hour and a half, the boy would talk about his friend by the riverside. The psychiatrist asked about school and about his relationship with his parents. She talked to the boy about the times when he was sad and when he was mad. She encouraged his parents to let him play with classmates outside of school, and hopefully that would help with his possible lonely behavior.

The boy started going out to parties and he was taken to parks and other events where there would be classmates. The boy had a lot of fun with his friends and he seemed to have no issue at all speaking to them. Once the family got home, however, the boy always paid a visit to the river until dinner was ready.

His parents had not wanted to resort to heeding their neighbor's advice. They found no harm initially in letting their son play by the river in the backyard. The water was shallow and they believed their son was very careful. However, since the arrival of the River Girl, his parents became more and more anxious. They were not superstitious people, so that made no links to the five-year-old blonde girl that drowned ten years ago. They were sure that there was something in their son's mind that had decided to act out as it was. Until they could find a cure, they set up a chain-link fence around their yard, separating them from the river.

When their son came home from school and found the fence there, he cried himself to sleep. The parents were baffled by their son's devotion to this imaginary friend in the river. Would they have to move in order for things to get better? The son tried to stop crying so they wouldn't make him move away.

The following day, the son snuck out with his coat and boots late at night to talk to his friend the River Girl. He didn't know why his mom and dad were so strict against him being with her. She was the first friend he ever made, and besides, she was lonely without him.

"Your mommy and daddy put up this fence," The girl pouted. The boy sat on the other side of the fence and looked at her.

"Maybe because they can't see you," The boy suggested.

"They can't," she put her small arms around herself. "They can't see me because, it's because they don't want to see me. But they can see me if they want to, I'm right here!" She cried.

"They said that if I try to play with you anymore, then they're going to make me move," the boy admitted.

The girl wailed, "Why don't your mommy and daddy want us to be friends? It's not fair I don't have any friends. You're my only friend. Other than you I don't have any more."

"I know," the boy looked down. "I can't stay here long. If they catch me out here, I'm going to be in big trouble."

"Can't you just, why won't you just run away? That's what I did." The girl floated a little farther downstream. "I ran far away, and now I can do whatever I want to. You should come with me so you can do whatever you want."

"I don't want to make mommy sad though," the boy told the

River Girl. "If I ran away, she would cry a lot. And daddy would be really mad."

The little girl looked away and put her hands to her face. She started to cry. "You don't wanna be my friend anymore."

"No, I do!" the boy stood up from his spot. "I do wanna be friends, but, if mommy and daddy catch me then we can't be friends anymore. And I don't want to make them sad. But I still wanna be friends." The boy squeezed his hand and a bit of his arm through the fence, reaching out to her. "I really like being friends with you, okay? Don't be sad."

The girl still cried, but she nodded. Her crying eventually slowed down and she sniffed. "Do you think they'll let us be friends if I give you your toys back?"

"Maybe," the boy recalled how it was his disappearing toys that made his parents start keeping him away from the River Girl in the first place. "But you said that you would bring them back anyway," he reminded her.

"I will," she said. "I'm almost done playing with them and then, then I'll give them back."

As far as his parents knew, the boy stopped visiting the river. The boy would go out at night instead, or very early in the morning before his parents ever woke up. He would talk with the River Girl about school and he would tell her jokes. One day, she brought back the triceratops. "You can have this back now." The paint was worn out by the river, but otherwise it was still in good shape. The boy was a little upset that his triceratops lost color, but he was also just very glad to have it back. The little girl put it at the edge of the bank so the boy's parents could get it when they woke up. She still had some of his soldiers and a toy car, but she promised to give them back as well later. "Thank you for being my friend," the little girl said that night.

"You're welcome," the boy said. He was not yet old enough to think of to say 'and thank you for being mine.'

That morning, the boy asked his mother to get his toy triceratops from the other side of the fence. The mother, still waking up and a little confused, asked him how the toy triceratops ended up there. "The River Girl brought it back," he told her.

A jolt of panic went through the mother's spine. She had thought that the talk about the River Girl was over. "That's it," she told her son. "I don't want to hear you talk about the River Girl ever again, do you hear me?"

"But mom," the boy pleaded.

"No 'buts'! You are forbidden to ever talk about her ever again! If you do, we are moving."

"No, mommy, don't make me move!" the boy shouted. He didn't want the little girl to be lonely anymore.

"Then stop talking about the River Girl, there is no River Girl."

"There is a River Girl," the boy complained, and shouted over his mother's shouting, "You just don't see her 'cause you don't want to see her, but she's right there!"

When the boy pointed over to the river, the mother thought she saw something at the corner of her eye. When she looked, she felt a wave of relief at seeing nothing there. "That's it," she warned. "No more talk about the River Girl, do you understand?"

The boy crossed his arms and scowled. He didn't answer his mother, but she took his silence as an affirmation. Once her son went to school, the mother walked around the house to retrieve the triceratops. 'You just don't see her 'cause you don't want to see her.' She was shouting for him to be quiet or get in trouble when he screamed it to her, but now the accusation was crisp in her mind. The mother looked on to the river, making her way towards the plastic toy. She tried to think of how the triceratops could have gotten back there, she thought she looked everywhere the day she spent hours along the bank.

The mother had the toy triceratops in her hand when she dared to try and see the River Girl. The mother looked out into the river for a while, trying to imagine what the River Girl would look like. Slowly, in her mind's eye, she imagined a little girl with blue eyes and long blond hair, in the river barefoot with a tattered nightgown. The child was only a baby, about four, perhaps five years old.

As soon as she realized that her image was getting too much into detail, she thought she saw a flash of something in the water. She saw for a brief second a little girl with blue eyes, blond hair and a nightgown.

The mother turned and ran as fast as she could inside the house, panting. She closed all the shutters going towards the river. She wouldn't let the boy open any of the shutters to the back until the feeling of being watched had faded from her thought, which wasn't until her husband got home and she went to work.

She never got the chance to explain what happened, but the father could tell something was wrong with how shaken up she was before going to work. He went to the backyard shutters and opened them again. Was it something about the back yard? Did it have something to do with the river, perhaps? He turned to his son who was playing with the triceratops that had faded paint.

"Hey pal, you found it," his father smiled. "Looks like you might have found it outside. Where was it?"

"It wasn't lost, daddy," the boy muttered. "Mommy says I'm not allowed to talk about it."

"I see," the father nodded. He decided to drop the subject for now, and sat with his son in front of the television for most of the afternoon. The two decided to watch a movie and the father had made some popcorn for them to eat until the mother came home. Once she did, the parents started cooking dinner together while the boy snuck into the back yard.

The father looked over to his wife. "How was work?" he asked.

"Fine," she responded. Her husband walked up to her and hugged her from behind.

"Are you going to tell me what's wrong?" he cooed. "What happened while I was at work?"

The mother told him everything that happened with the triceratops at the other end of the fence. She told him what their son said about not seeing the River Girl, but she left out having tried it herself and getting too scared to continue further. "This place isn't too good with our minds," the father decided. "Maybe we should move."

"We can't actually move," the mother sighed. "We don't have enough money to. And finding a good place to live with decent rent will take weeks.

"We'll figure something out," the father assured. It was then that their son walked into the house. He looked angrily at his mother.

"You didn't say 'thank you,'" he murmured.

His mother had chills go up her spine. "Excuse me? What did you say to me?"

"You didn't thank my friend for bringing my toy back! She thought you would be nicer if she brought back my toy but she says you only stared at her and ran away."

"I didn't," the mother began to say. "I thought we weren't

going to talk about her anymore," she reminded him sternly.

"She only wanted to play with me, why are you always so mean to her? I hate you!" he shouted before turning and running up to his room.

"You get back here young man, that's no way to talk to your mother!" the father shouted. He didn't come down, but instead slammed the door. Angry, the father ran up the stairs to have a talk with his son, and grounding him had come to mind. If anything, at least it would keep him out of the river for a week.

The mother was frozen. Her son was inside at the time, so how could he know what she did or didn't do when she was out there? She felt her stomach lurch and she looked out the back door where the river was. The silhouette of a small girl in the river was much easier to see at night, or perhaps it was the wife's imagination.

Even as she looked out the back door, thinking about what had happened on that day, the mother was starting to become desperate to save her son from whatever waited for him by the riverside. Could it be possible that there really was a spirit waiting for her son there? While her two boys were upstairs, cautiously, she made her way to the back yard.

The mother bundled up in her jacket, but it was still getting too cold for normal jackets. Snowfall was expected in the week. Her teeth chattered, but she was determined to walk over to the fence. She looked into the black river, the stars in the sky provided comfort, but not as much as the inviting porch light to her house. She could run inside and not think about it. It felt silly to stand there. Silly and frightening. "Hello," she whispered.

"I don't know if you're really there…" Why was she out here? What did she hope to accomplish, throwing words to an empty river?

But what if it wasn't empty?

"I wanted to thank you for bringing my son's triceratops back. I'm sorry that I didn't thank you before. He talks about you a lot, and he really cares about you. He's such a good kid," the mother sniffed, her voice wavering from the cold and the wave of emotions she was feeling. "He didn't start making friends at school until he became friends with you. We were concerned he wouldn't make friends at all. So thank you. But please."

At some point, the mother had started crying. She had to speak up so that she could be heard through her own crying. "Please don't take our son away from us! If I ever lost my son I would go crazy. We love him. We want him to have a long, happy life so please don't take him away. We need him here. We love our son. Please don't take him away."

Soon after, the mother sank to her knees and tried to wipe away the tears from her eyes. She didn't feel afraid anymore. Aside from the rushing river, everything was silent. The mother tried to compose herself before going into the house, and it was then that she noticed the snow had started to fall.

Dinner was eaten quietly between the three. After dinner, the boy was sent up to brush his teeth and go to sleep. He slept soundly, and his parents curled together to sleep while the winter snow fell gently onto the naked ground.

The next morning, the mother was the first to wake up. She dragged her feet down the stairs to make some coffee.

She reached the bottom of the stairs. Her eyes caught a glance out the back yard through the sliding glass window, and she could clearly see the image of a young girl, no older than five, bending down at the bank of the river to set something down. The mother kept staring at the little girl who straightened up and caught the eye of the woman. The little girl shyly waved at the mother, before fading from sight.

It took the mother a few moments to start walking again. She stared intently at the riverside every chance she got when making her coffee. While the coffee was brewing, the mother went up to get her coat, put on some snow boots, and walked to the backyard. She didn't want to go the fence by the river right away, but she willed her legs to keep walking. She shivered in the cold, but made it to the fence.

The mother almost cried out. There, lying between the bank and the fence was the rest of her son's toys. They were all worn out by the sun, but unharmed. There were no footsteps and no sign of disturbance in the snow except for the toys, which didn't have a snowflake on them. Somehow, the mother felt this was a sign. She didn't think she could not believe any more. The mother looked on into the river, nodded, and cried out, "Thank you so much."

By the riverside, there was a row of houses with the river in their backyards. One of the houses had a long metal pole where a fence used to be connected to. In that house lived a family that remembered the little girl that drowned in the river and how ten years later made good friends with the young man that lived there. They hadn't heard anything from her since their first winter, but they say 'hello' to the River Girl when they visit the back yard just in case she's still there.

UNDER THE BED

"I don't want to go to bed," Misty whined. She peeked over to her parents from her covers as she weakly protested bed time.

"That's too bad," her father replied. Her stepmother smiled and added, "How are you going to function tomorrow if you don't get any sleep tonight?"

"I don't need to sleep," Misty argued. Wait, don't leave me alone yet! What if there's something under my bed?"

Misty's stepmother walked over to Misty's bed and bent down to get a good look underneath. "Nothing down here but a family of dust bunnies," the stepmother confirmed. "It looks like they're getting ready for bed, too."

"Nothing in the closet, either," her father called out. "It looks like everything's just fine." He closed the closet door and Misty's stepmother straightened up from under the bed. "Now it's time for you to go to sleep, Misty," her father sighed.

Misty felt better now that the bed and closet had been checked. Still, she asked for them to leave a crack open on her door so the hallway light can shine through. This has been the pattern almost every night for putting Misty to bed. Sometimes she would ask for a story to help fall asleep, which her stepmother was very good at telling. She remembered the story of the dust bunnies, and thought about the story as she closed her eyes. The story of why dust bunnies live underneath little girl's beds.

There was a long time ago when all the dust bunnies in the dust bunny kingdom were happy. The king of the dust bunnies was adored by everyone who saw him. One day, there was a cloud that went over the land, and a great wind started to lift all the dust bunnies into a tornado.

"The tornado spun them round and round," Misty could hear her stepmother's voice. "Until they were left in a land of darkness, where everything was cramped and quiet. The dust bunnies that survived, including the king, feared the great tornado that took his subjects to such a dark and scary place. He started looking for a paradise; somewhere that the great tornado could not reach them. One day, his subjects found a cave. They waited in the cave quietly for the tornado to come back. Finally, they heard the 'vrooom' sound of the wind. It was coming closer, but the tornado could not reach them. Ever since that day, they have lived under beds away from the wind and the tornado."

"Mmh?" Misty stirred from her sleep. The sound of her stepmother's voice had left so suddenly from her mind that the silence woke her up. She didn't know what time it was, but she could tell it was very late. Misty peeked out of one of her eyes.

Staring at her with unblinking eyes, a hungry, jagged grin, was a pale gray-faced woman with eyes about ready to bulge out of her head. Her cheeks were sunken in. The little girl tried to scream, but failed at first. She panicked, tried to scream, but her throat wouldn't let her. She tried to move, but she was paralyzed. She watched with severe mortification as this woman figure slowly raised her bony, clawed hand towards Misty's chest.

Finally, she managed to scream. In an instant, the woman at the side of her bed went away. 'She's under me,' Misty thought in panic, and she screamed again.

Her father ran into the bedroom and turned on the light. "What, what is it, baby?" her father cried.

"Someone is under my bed!" She cried.

Her father sighed and rubbed his face. "Misty," he whined. But like a good father, he went to the bed and looked underneath anyway. "It's just the dust bunnies, Misty. Nothing here is going to hurt you."

"But I saw her, daddy," Misty insisted. "She was smiling really wide and her eyes were bulging out," she tried to continue but her father interrupted with a pat to her head.

"It was just a bad dream, sweetie," her father stood up and walked to her door. "I'm going to bed now, goodnight."

"But," Misty wanted to protest. She was too scared to go to sleep now, what if the things came back? The way her father stopped in the doorway, however, changed her mind. "Okay," she agreed hesitantly.

Misty was right in thinking that she wouldn't be able to sleep the rest of the night. The next morning, she was really tired when she went to school and fell asleep at her desk when doing homework. She was so tired that she fell asleep once at dinner. Misty's stepmother and father exchanged concerned glances, but decided to not say anything for now.

"Goodnight Misty," her stepmother and father said to her just as they were about to leave.

"Wait," Misty pleaded. "Will you look in the closet and under the bed?"

They did it just as they had every other night. 'Only dust bunnies,' the stepmother would say. 'Nothing at all' said the father. 'Tell me a story?' Misty asked her stepmother.

"Which one do you want to hear tonight?" she asked. "Is it the dust bunny one again?"

"No," Misty admitted. "Can you tell me a story about a woman who lives under the bed?"

The stepmother was a little taken aback, but determined for Misty to fall asleep, she had obliged. She was especially good at making up stories on the fly. "The story of the woman under the bed," she started.

"Once upon a time, there was a young woman who," the stepmother thought a moment. "Loved to sleep. She loved it so much, in fact, that everyone would call her 'Sleeping Beauty.' One night, she was laying down when she heard a knocking at her bedroom door. It was, ah," she thought a bit more. "The girl's parents. 'You sleep too much' they told her. 'You never go out and make friends. You have to go outside and make friends now, and don't come back until dark.' So she goes outside where all the kids are playing, but she doesn't find anyone who wants to play with her. She thinks about the nice dreams she has and wishes she was in her bed."

The stepmother was quiet for a minute, looking over at the father. "Ah," she exclaimed. "But near the end of the day, she met a boy named… Tommy. 'I've never seen you before,' Tommy said to the girl. 'That's because I'm usually in my bed sleeping,' the girl replied. 'Well you can't make very many friends doing that, what's so special about sleeping?' 'Oh, lots of things,' said the little girl. 'And you can too make friends when you're asleep. I dream about many friends. I'm the most popular person ever in my dreams.' Tommy was very interested in this little girl's passion about dreams."

"Did they become friends?" Misty asked. The stepmom was quick to nod. "Oh yes, the best of friends," she affirmed. "The two of them spent a lot of time together after that. Tommy and the little girl would spend a lot of time in either of their bedrooms, talking and laughing and playing games. The little girl talked about the dreams she had to Tommy, and Tommy would talk about his dreams to her. The little girl's dreams seemed a lot more exciting, but they enjoyed each other's company nonetheless. Until…"

"Until what," Misty squeaked.

The stepmom realized she wrote herself into a corner. Misty was right, until what? She hadn't mentioned why the little girl started going under the bed. "Until," the stepmother decided. "Tommy got really sick."

"Tommy was in his bed for weeks. And his friend, the little girl, was so worried about him she would often hide under his bed so neither of their parents would make her leave. The little girl would come out after the parents were away, hold Tommy's hand, and tell him that he was going to be okay. She bet he had a lot of really great dreams. After a while, Tommy was ready to go up to heaven. He asked the little girl if she would make friends and give them good dreams like she did for him. She promised she would, and then Tommy went to sleep forever. So," the stepmother tried to end on a good note. "For every good boy and girl, there's a little girl under their bed that comes out when they're sleeping to make sure they have good dreams, and only wants to be friends with them."

"The girl under the bed only wants to be friends?" Misty repeated. She felt a little bad for screaming now, and hoped that she might get a chance to see the girl again and apologize. There was still a part of her though that was terrified of seeing the woman again.

Misty's father and stepmother left the door cracked open, the closet closed, and the hallway light on. Misty fell asleep while thinking about the story her stepmother told her. It helped her calm down enough to sleep even though she was still nervous about the girl. 'She's just lonely and misses Tommy,' she'd tell herself, and those thoughts helped her fall asleep.

She woke up again by the sudden silence. Misty was too groggy to remember the girl under her bed, and when she turned her head to the side, the girl wasn't there. Misty turned her head towards the darkness, past her feet, and her mind went into a panic again.

There was the girl. She wasn't smiling. Instead, her mouth was open as though she was screaming in agony. Her limbs were long and bony, and reaching for Misty's leg. The closet door was wide open, and it was as though it was slow motion that the creature was moving. Misty's chest tightened, the grotesque and terrifying sight coming back to her in a wave of panic. 'Go away,' she wanted to scream, but her voice wouldn't come out. She tried screaming again to scare the thing away but still no sound came out. Misty closed her eyes and tried with all her might to scream.

It was a weak scream, but it was noise nonetheless. It motivated her to try more, and she was able to scream louder. She opened her eyes to see that the girl was in mid-crawl from her bed to the closet door. She was moving backwards, almost gliding back into the closet. The closet door was closed without a sound just as her stepmother hurried inside. "Misty, what is it?" she cried.

Misty couldn't speak she was so horrified. Her mouth opened and closed a few times, and her stepmother turned on the light. "Misty what's wrong?" her stepmother looked over to the closet door which Misty was looking at. Her stepmother was a little wary about what could have terrified Misty so much, so she was cautious in opening the closet door. The closet light was turned on and all the shirts and coats were pushed aside. Her stepmother checked every bit of the closet but couldn't find anything.

During the search, Misty had managed to find her voice. "The girl, she was in the closet! She was crawling and she tried to grab me, she was screaming, but no voice was coming out, her arm was really thin-."

"Misty calm down," her stepmother implored. She closed the closet door and walked to the foot of Misty's bed to try to soothe her. "You're just having another bad dream." Still, two in a row made her stepmother anxious. "Do you want to sleep in the bed with my and your father tonight? Will that make you feel better?"

Misty nodded and wiped the tears from her eyes. She started to cry and her stepmother embraced the young girl, picking her up and taking her to the parent's bedroom.

Misty slept between her two parents that night. She was worried about falling asleep at first, but because she didn't get a full night's sleep last night it was impossible for her to keep her eyes open. She slept soundly with them and didn't wake up until later, when her stepmother got out of bed to go to work. Her father worked at home editing journals for a local magazine, and her stepmother was one of the journalists. Misty liked the other bedtime story about how her father and stepmother met. She didn't remember a time with her real mother, so it was as though she never actually had one. Her stepmother talked about how her father was a sports journalist editor until after a bunch of houses blew up when Misty was a few months old.

Sometimes Misty wanted to ask about her mother, but she was worried that it might make her father sad.

Misty felt well-rested now and got up before her father did. She hadn't been in her father's room since she can remember. She was old enough now to walk on her own, and after a bit of looking around she found a box of portraits. Most of them were for work. A lot of pictures were of riots or people chaining their arms together. There were signs being waved and buildings with broken windows.

She noticed after a little while that there was one folder that was kept apart from the others. She looked at the pictures. There was a blown-up Health center, a few other blown up buildings that looked like important offices, and then random pictures of people. She couldn't tell which pictures happened when, but a lot of them were pictures of people smiling with families and friends.

She saw a few pictures with her dad in them, but he looked a lot younger. He was with people she didn't recognize. Some of them wore hats, and some of the women had pretty scarves around their head. She giggled at her father's afro. As she went through these pictures, there was an old piece of paper that fell through her fingers. She went to pick it up.

Her eyes widened, and her mouth hung open. "Daddy," she screamed without thinking.

Her father shot out of bed and rubbed his face violently. "What," he shouted back without meaning to.

Misty picked up the picture and ran to her father, putting the picture in his hands. "Honey, you shouldn't be looking at those pictures they're too gruesome," he scolded. "You don't just go around looking into other people's things."

"Look, daddy!" Misty pointed to the picture she gave him.

Misty's father took the drawing that his daughter found in his possessions. He felt a lump in his chest, "Where did you find this?"

Her father's voice was grave, almost seething. She shrank a little bit. "Um," she muttered.

"Put it back. Put this back right now, don't look into my things," he demanded.

"But it's her, daddy," Misty exclaimed. "It's the girl from under the bed and in the closet."

"I said put it back!"

Misty jumped. Her father rarely yelled at her, and she felt herself about to cry. She slunk back to the box with all the pictures in it and put everything back. She was crying, but trying to do so silently so as not to get yelled at again by her father.

While Misty was putting everything back, her father was rubbing his face with his hand. The hand ended over his open mouth before setting his hand to his side with a sigh. "Misty," he spoke softly. "Come here girl."

Misty looked over at her father and wiped the tears from her eyes. She crawled into the bed with him and he hugged her on his lap. "I think that it's time that I tell you something about your mother."

Misty sat snug in her dad's arms. She could hear his heartbeat, and it helped calm her down. She wiped the last of her tears from her eyes. "You're too young to understand the details, but all around the world people do not like other people. A lot of times it's for things that would otherwise be minor details about a person. There are some people, for example, who don't like us because of our skin." Misty's father held out his daughter's darkly-colored hand. "Some people didn't like your mother because of where she was from. Those people made a health center blow up where she worked."

Misty's father took a deep sigh. "Well, before all that happened, your mother used to love reading about mythologies from different places. There is one spirit she started talking about that would take and eat people with corruption in their hearts. It was a woman that hid in dark places until you slept somewhere alone. Now, after your mother died, I had given up on my job to start a new one so I could expose what happened to your mother. But my bosses 'urged' me to revise a few things in the story. They said it was for everyone's safety. So I could write the story of what happened, or I could write it with a bunch of changes and make it into a completely different story." Misty's father was silent for a moment. "I chose the wrong story."

Misty didn't understand much, but she knew that her father was really sad about her mother's death. Misty knew something bad happened. "Your stepmother was a friend of mine at the time, and when I started having nightmares of the woman from the myths trying to take me away, she suggested that I have the woman drawn to sort of get her out of my head. After a while, right around the time I started dating your stepmom and she was living here, I thought the spirit had gone away for good."

The story sounded scary, and Misty felt a chill go up her spine. She curled closer into her father. What her father didn't say was that he suspected the same spirit was going after his daughter because she couldn't get a grip on him. "The woman is just a nightmare, Misty. She can't hurt you; I promise."

"Was mommy a nice person?" Misty asked. It was one of the questions she was always too afraid to ask her father, but now it was an opportunity.

"Yes baby, she was a very nice person who loved you very much." His heart panged to think of her again. He hoped the shame of his decision would disappear over time, but now the consequences were after his daughter.

"Did she tell stories like mommy does?" she asked.

"No, she was very quiet. She didn't talk very much but she loved to hear me talking. She wasn't into sports but she listened anyway. She would read a lot, and only say small things about what she was reading. She asked a lot of questions though."

"Do you still miss her?" Misty looked up at her dad's face. The hair on his chin tickled her forehead.

"Yes I do, very much. But she would want me to move on. We both knew you needed a mommy and a daddy, and she liked your stepmom when she was alive. Just because I fell in love again doesn't mean I don't love your mother anymore. And we all love you." He looked down and kissed her forehead.

Later that night, the family of three had dinner together, and Misty's stepmother and father went together to finish the dishes while Misty went into the living room to watch television. "What's wrong, Thomas," Misty's stepmother asked. "You look a little shaken."

"Kelsey, do you remember the nightmares I was having when we both met? I think that Misty is starting to have those nightmares. I can't help but feel responsible."

"Oh baby, it's not your fault. It's a bit weird, but it isn't your fault at all. When Misty was talking about the girl I actually had a suspicion. Misty's description was the same as yours back then. But I didn't want to say anything because I didn't want to bring back painful memories for you."

"It's more painful knowing that Misty is dealing with the nightmares at all. You know I've always been skeptical of the spirit stuff, but what if it's true? What if there's a spirit trying to pay me back for what I did six years ago?"

"You didn't have a choice," Kelsey insisted.

"No I did," Thomas replied. "And I made the wrong decision. I chose money over the truth, and a lot of families suffered because of it."

"You're being silly," Kelsey sighed. "There is no such thing as spirits. It's maybe the nightmares of a guilty conscience and the guilt maybe somehow rubbed off on Misty. There's no way that there's a vengeful spirit out to get you."

"Well I'm going to find out," Thomas concluded.

That night, as they were tucking Misty into bed, her father suggested that Misty and her stepmom sleep together for the night. "I want to sleep on my own tonight, just to check something out. Besides, it might be more relaxing for Misty to sleep with someone, right?"

Misty agreed, though her stepmother was curious over what her husband was hoping to do on his own. "Sleep well," she told him regardless. "I'll see you in the morning."

Misty hugged and kissed her father goodnight. Her stepmother hugged him next, whispering, "Are you sure about this?"

"Maybe you're right," he admitted. "It could just be me. The best way to get rid of your demons is to face them, so that's what I'm going to do."

The night fell over the town. Crickets chirped and frogs croaked outside, and a guilty man lay alone in his bed for the first time in six years. He sighed and rolled over, trying to think of work or of tomorrow or anything that didn't have to do with the spirit his late wife told him about. He thought about the riots and protests he's been covering, trying to make up for the injustice he did to his wife's memory years ago. He only wanted a safe life for his daughter, he reasoned. It was all he ever really wanted.

Nearly an hour passed before he felt his eyes becoming heavy. He dreamed about shapes and colors, and he heard voices, but they never really made sense. He thought he saw shapes that were similar to snowflakes, but they warped and shaped as though he were looking through a kaleidoscope. Noises were incoherent, as they changed to distorted pieces of music and sounds of the city.

He heard whispering, but couldn't make out what anyone was whispering about.

Thomas woke up, not remembering a thing from what he dreamed but was startled by the sudden silence of the room.

He was awake, but his eyes were firmly closed. He felt dizzy and tried to move his hands, but found he could not. He tried as best as he could to forget the feeling of being watched. If he could sleep through the whole night without looking at the woman, maybe the spirit would find it useless to torment him.

There was no such luck. Thomas couldn't find the fatigue to fall asleep, and the feeling of being watched became too strong. He wanted to speak, or maybe even to apologize, but he couldn't speak or do anything vocally. Maybe just a peek, she probably wasn't there anyway.

When Thomas managed to open his eyes, looming over him with its face inches from his was the woman. Her bulging eyes stared through him, her mouth filled with jagged teeth, opened wide as though shrieking out of pure terror. Her sunken cheeks and pale gray complexion brought the man's memories back to the image of the corpses he had seen six years ago. He tried to scream, yet his lungs forbade it. Anyway, there was no use screaming, he was too far gone now.

The spirit's lanky arms gripped the man at his shoulders. Her sharp claws dug cleanly into the flesh of his forearms as she claimed him against his wishes as her prize for patience. He kept trying to move, to scream, to call for help, but as his body thumped on the ground and was dragged under the bed, his body frozen with both sleep and fear, his attempts for escape were futile. He thought of the horrible thing he had done which ate away at him, and now it had consumed him for good.

When Misty woke up the next morning, she saw her stepmother sound asleep beside her. She smiled, having had no nightmares the whole night. She wanted to tell her dad how it worked, so she hurried to his room.

As she opened the door to her father's bedroom, she felt as though the air was a little too cold. She turned to her father's bed, but he wasn't there. The sheets were tossed aside, so she wondered if he was awake already. She hurried to the kitchen but he was missing. Misty tried to look everywhere, but he was nowhere in the house. His car was still parked in the driveway.

Misty cried out for her stepmother, who jolted out of bed. She looked around her, and remembering what happened last night she ran out to where Misty waited, tears in her eyes. She couldn't find her father. The stepmother looked everywhere as well, fearing what might have happened she also looked under their bed and in the closet to no avail. They filed for a missing person report as soon as they could, but there had never been a trace of him. Misty's stepmother took her in, but even though Misty would never know the whole story, there was always a little bit in her stepmother's mind that would wonder. She would think for a moment, then with a shudder and a light cry, hide the possibility deep into her mind.

LOST IN THE WOODS

Camping was Amelia's favorite thing to do. When she was young her parents would take her, her older sister and her younger brother out into the campsites and they would bond like she supposed all family members did. There was something tranquil about being surrounded by nature.

She would always suggest to her friends that they could all go out hiking and camping, but a lot of them felt wary from being away from their modern comforts for long. She supposed that they felt lonely when they weren't directly connected in one form or another to the internet. Amelia never had that problem. She loved the isolation, and besides, the forest itself was great company.

There were a few friends that shared her enthusiasm with nature. Prin was a quirky young woman who adored nature. She would spend a lot of her time trying to identify birds and trees. Amelia would be the poor soul who would be forced to listen to Prin talk about every plant and bird and why they were all so different and important. It didn't interest Amelia a whole lot what the plants and birds were so long as she got to be surrounded by them. Jonah was another friend who adored nature, though he found comfort in the paved paths of walks already taken. Amelia preferred the unruly nature, but for as long as she's traveled, it seemed that no matter how far Amelia would go she was never far enough away to escape civilization.

"I have the same problem," Amelia's friend Shawnese took a bite of her pumpkin pie while the two sat at a diner after one of their hikes. "See the thing about it is, right? That I always end up on the border of one area or private property or another when I'm hunting. I'm tracking a deer or rabbit and after a while it seems like the best game is sitting in someone's back yard."

"Sounds annoying."

"It is," Shawnese exclaimed. "A lot of the people don't use that land anyway, why does everything have to be owned?"

"I don't know," Amelia replied absently. She looked out the window towards the sea of forest and mountain, but even from this far she could see the gleam of windows hiding behind the branches.

"You should go hunting with me sometime. Prin is vegetarian

and Jonah is an asshole who'll scare all the animals away."

Amelia chuckled a little, but her eyes never left the window. "I don't think I'm comfortable shooting a gun, but maybe I'll come watch sometime."

The two girls were silent for a few seconds. "This is really bothering you that you can't go anywhere unexplored, huh?"

Amelia sighed. "No, not really. It's fine."

Shawnese threw a fry at her friend, who turned her head in surprise. Shawnese held up another fry as a warning. "Don't lie to me, girl. You gonna tell me what's up or are we gonna have some fighting words?"

"Alright," Amelia laughed a little before eating the fry Shawnese tossed at her. "You're right, I guess. I just wish I could go somewhere where I'm not within sight, sound or smell of humanity. I want to be able to go out somewhere and get a real feeling of nature. The woods around here feel like they're shrinking, I've been everywhere. I want to get out there into somewhere that's never been discovered. But everything's been found already out there. I don't think there's an inch of land that's not claimed somehow."

"Wish I could help, Amelia," Shawnese replied. "Have you told Prin about it? Maybe she knows somebody."

"Somebody to what?" Amelia asked.

"There's gotta be places 'somewhere' not yet explored, right? Prin's family travels a lot, right? Maybe they'll know of somewhere."

"I don't really know if she'll know anyone that is as much into nature as I am. Besides, even if there was a place how would I get the money and the time off work to go out to wherever it was if it existed?"

"Jonah's got money, and he's got the wanderlust almost as bad as you do. And even if he decides not to, I'll help you raise the money."

"Wow Shawnese that's really great of you," Amelia smiled. She really did have the best friends.

"Don't thank me too much, I get paid dirt in retail. Still, I'd love to help you out."

"Well anything is a step up. Anyway, I seriously doubt there's anywhere we'll be able to go. It's all been done before. Maybe I'll just drive to the valley where it's more open next time."

Shawnese shrugged, "Whatever you say, girl. Just stop moping around though. I get upset seeing you like that for real. Smile more."

Amelia gave her friend a crooked, goofy smile. "I said a smile, dammit," Shawnese threw another fry at Amelia as the girls laughed.

Weeks went by and Amelia's mood didn't change too much. Her desire for something new burned into her soul. She hoped she could find relief in the valley, but everywhere she went was still familiar to her and didn't provide relief for very long.

Amelia had made good friends with Shawnese, Jonah and Prin in college seven years back and the four of them were very close. Despite their branching paths throughout their education the four of them kept in touch through all of it. There were other friends, but when life greeted any of them with pain or pleasure, it was the other three in the circle who would know about it first. Amelia wasn't surprised, therefore, when Jonah came up to her house to have a talk.

"So, I heard you had some wanderlust blues?" Jonah asked just as Amelia answered the door.

"Good to see you, Jonah," Amelia responded. "I'm guessing Shawnese told you about it."

"Actually, Prin did but I think she heard it from Shawnese."

"Fantastic."

"Why didn't you tell us about it, Amelia? We could totally hook something up I think if you really wanna go," Jonah gave Amelia a wide smile. "Prin's got that grandpa who's traveled the world, he might know of somewhere. And I can get us some tickets somewhere no problem. You have like a week's worth of sick days, don't you? You never get sick; you won't be needing them the rest of the year."

Amelia simultaneously hated and was relieved at Jonah's ability to make her excited for a trip she felt was practically impossible. "I don't know," she admitted.

"Look, you work too hard. Prin works too hard. Shawnese works too hard and I'm too bored. I think this would be a really nice trip for all of us. We're all still young, no kids, no health problems, nothing but our jobs weighing us down and even then, one little week away won't hurt anyone."

"I agree with Jonah," Prin piped up from her bedroom. Amelia and Prin had been roommates since Prin graduated from college. It made things harder when Amelia felt the need to hide away from Prin's barrage of plant and bird facts. For now, it made things hard for Amelia to get away from the whole idea of going somewhere without human habitation.

Prin picked up on Amelia's hesitation, and it concerned her. "Amelia, you act as though you don't really want to go anywhere new."

"It isn't that," Amelia sighed. "It's just," honestly, she didn't know what it was. There was just something nagging on her at the back of her mind as a sign that this was a bad idea.

"Amelia, you're the most adventurous of all of us. I thought you would be a lot more excited about this, honestly. Where's that sense of unbridled bravery you have? Where's the Passion and the nagging voice that says 'get up,' 'do something,' 'Try something new?' You're always so excited about stuff like this," Prin urged.

"I don't really know myself," Amelia confessed. "Something just seems off."

Prin walked out of her room. "Well I was talking to my grandfather about mysterious forests that he might know about his travel. He did mention the sort of forest that's right in our country, though we'd have to travel to the other side of it. The forest is called 'lost forest,' have you ever heard of it?"

"Lost forest?" Jonah chuckled. "No, I haven't heard of it."

"It's filled with Douglas Fir and cardinals," Prin explained. "I researched it. Apparently, it's a forest that not many people know about except for a green patch in the map. The reason being the locals try keep it as secret as they can. It's believed that once you step foot into the forest, it's impossible to find your way back. The natives there told my grandpa it was tradition to give tribute to the forest spirits in order to bring back long lost travelers, and the story is that the few that survive find their way by following a river made of silver."

"Sounds spooky," Jonah grinned. "I think I'll stay in the village where it's safe. But you guys should go hike there, it sounds awesome."

"What's the point in going if you won't hike with us?" Amelia asked.

"It's vacation with my friends," Jonah grinned. "You wouldn't be spending ALL your time hiking anyway, would you?"

"I beg to differ," Amelia confessed. She had to admit, going to this place sounded like a great opportunity, and potentially sating her wander lust would give her a huge piece of mind.

After a few months of planning and waiting for the perfect fall weather to go on their trip, the four friends were ready to go.

"I'm so excited," Shawnese cheered. "This is gonna be so much fun, just us, and nature. Too bad there's no hunting on this trip but that's a small detail. What's this tribe like, Prin?"

The two sat together in the plane, while Amelia and Jonah shared a seating lane behind the other two girls. Everyone was chatting and excited except for Amelia who kept looking down from the window at the land below. Everything looked patterned from the sky, not a single wild arrangement to be seen all across the country.

The scenery changed about ten minutes away from their destination. There was a huge area of nothing but forest. It looked like it may be a national park, but it was so vast that Amelia was sure it would have to be the biggest national park in the world.

Everyone was tired from the flight when they finally landed. Jonah arranged for the four of them to stay in a hotel across the village so that they could visit whenever they like, but more to the point, they could stay close to the forest.

"Where's the forest?" Jonah said to the group as they arrived in a gimmick-like voice.

"Oh no, it's lost!" Prin replied with a giggle. The two of them laughed as though they were the cleverest people in the world.

The four of them walked from the small airport to the hotel carrying a week's worth of luggage and hiking supplies. There was a grocery store where they could buy snacks and bottles for the trip, and it was just on the outskirts of village property. The hotel had two rooms; one for Jonah which was much smaller, and the three girls got a three-bedroom suite. It wasn't super fancy, but Jonah wanted to make sure that everyone would be comfortable nonetheless.

Amelia was already lifting her spirits. The sight of the seemingly endless sight of forest filled her with determination, and she couldn't wait to set foot into it.

After the girls set their things down into the hotel, Amelia smiled more than she had all summer. "Let's go," she said.

"What, now?" Prin sighed. "But we just got here."

"You're not tired after spending eight hours in a plane, Amelia? The sun is already setting; can't we go tomorrow morning?"

"We came here to hike, right?" Amelia insisted. "So, we should go hike. We should go explore and see what the Lost Forest has to offer."

"That's the thing," Jonah chimed in from the doorway. He had all his things tossed into the room down the hall. "People already get lost in those woods, right? So, let's not test faith and start bright and early tomorrow instead. I personally would feel much better in the daylight than I would at night."

The other two agreed, and Amelia was left huffing and putting her things away. The group settled down for some breakfast and went to bed. Amelia, however, couldn't sleep. She looked over to where the village was. It was as though the end of life started in the village. Once everyone was settled into their homes, nothing stirred. Not even a lantern glowed. From the vantage point of a two-story window she could look onward to the forest. It was much larger than she had imagined. She was sure that she would be let down, and the Lost Forest wouldn't be the same as it was when Prin's grandfather visited the area. Amelia marveled at how dark it was. She looked up and saw the stars, but even through the hotel lights she could tell there were more stars than they could see in the city.

The cicadas outside and Prin's light snoring was the only noise Amelia could hear. Everything else was like a void. It was more soothing than what Amelia had anticipated. A few hours more and Amelia couldn't fight the sleep anymore. She crawled into bed and fell asleep as soon as her ear hit the cool pillow. She sighed, feeling much better over the whole adventure. She was so glad that her friends talked her into this, despite the feeling of warning at the back of her mind.

The next morning, the group ate a big breakfast at the hotel's diner. They chatted excitedly over what they planned on doing during this vacation. Prin wanted to get a look at the birds and trees that were indigenous at this part of the continent, Jonah was interested in hearing some folklore from the villagers, Shawnese was interested in knowing about the kinds of animals that were in this area, and Amelia was just excited to get into the woods. She would be lying if she hadn't confessed to herself that a part of her hoped to get lost, at least for a little bit. She was a bit eager for the feeling of isolation, of complete spiritual synchronization with nature.

At long last, the friends geared up for the hike and wandered through the village. Amelia was too excited, but Shawnese noticed the odd looks that the four were getting on their way to the forest. 'They probably aren't used to visitors,' she supposed.

"Wait, travelers," a man's voice gained up to them on the dirt road. "Where are you going, don't you know the forest is dangerous?"

"Dangerous?" Jonah turned around with the others. "How so?"

"The forest is sacred," the man explained. "It is not kind to people, it will try to keep you lost in it forever. The trees and paths change so that you cannot find your way back. I am telling you, you cannot go in there."

"But we came all this way," Prin explained. "Could we maybe at least arrange a tour inside, just a hike along the border?"

Amelia's body tensed. No, that was not the experience she had wanted. The man seemed hesitant to agree, but did so in the end. "There is a man who has traveled into the forest many times, he can guide you a little bit but you must come back quickly before the forest is aware of your presence."

The man had left to find the person who can tour them, and Amelia turned bitterly to the others. "We can't just be here to be babysat into the forest."

"It's their rules," Shawnese shrugged. "They probably have a good reason for it."

"At least we can get into the forest. I know it's not exactly what you wanted Amelia, but it's still somewhere new." Prin gave her friend a supportive smile. "Maybe we can find another place sometime next year; somewhere where we can have the real experience."

The man returned with a guide who was five-and-a-half feet tall and lanky. He wore a t-shirt and shorts with sandals, and he seemed quite interested in the newcomers. His accent was so thick it was hard to understand, but Jonah especially was good at making it out.

"So, what's so sacred about this forest?" Jonah asked the man.

"Dis forest," the man began. "Many spirit, stay away from human. Very very dangerous for people. Lost brother eight-eighteen year. Lost many people. It will change to confuse you."

"But you were able to get out alive?" Jonah asked.

"Ah was very lucky. Figure guide me, silver path led me out. It was my wife's prayer to save me."

When they reached the forest, the guide took out a ball of twine. He tied one end of twine four yards away from the forest on a pole that was possibly placed there for this reason, and he breached the first trees of the forest. "Come, hurry, do not want to be behind."

The group of friends stayed close to the guide. Prin was having a great time naming the different plants and marveling at the three or four she didn't know. Jonah kept talking to the guide about the secrets of the forest, though there was very little that the tribesman would tell an outsider, since a lot of the stories were sacred. He did, however, share a lot of jokes and his own story about his family quite readily. Shawnese became interested in some imprints on the ground. She muttered about the prints looking like deer prints but bigger, and they were a little 'off.'

Amelia kept quiet, stewing in her bitterness, wanting to just leave the party and run off into the woods on her own. She felt the light wind through the leaves, as though it were a whisper, 'come closer.' She was confident in her sense of direction, of course she wouldn't get lost. Besides, at the very worst she had a compass in her backpack. She gripped the shoulder straps of the pack and, watching her friends, slowly backing up into the forest. She went until she couldn't see anyone, and farther still until she couldn't hear anyone.

"Amelia don't you remember," Prin started. She turned to notice that Amelia wasn't where she had been moments ago. She could easily see the guide, Jonah and Shawnese but she didn't see Amelia at all. "Shawnese, Jonah, do you see Amelia anywhere?"

Shawnese felt a sudden rise in her throat. She looked around for Amelia, and even went so far as to go deeper in until she could only see Prin, but she hurried back in a panic. "Amelia's gone!"

"I had warned," the guide shook his head gravely. "She is now lost."

"Lost, no she can't be lost," Jonah protested. He called out for Amelia, but she didn't answer. He started to head forward into the forest, but Prin stopped him. "No use in you getting lost too, Jonah."

"What else are we supposed to do," Jonah demanded.

"Not'ing to do but wait," the guide sighed deeply. He seemed somberly indifferent to the loss of another human to the forest.

"You have to have like a rescue team or something," Shawnese insisted. "You can't expect us to just wait and see whether or not our friend turns into animal chow, do you?"

"It is will of spirits now, if she is spared."

Amelia's friends left the forest to look for someone who would go in and look for Amelia. The three of them thought to go in together to find their lost friend, but once it was found what they wanted to do they were not allowed back into the forest. They tried to run in, but some of the villagers that were concerned for the outsiders and the state of the Lost Forest kept them pushed back. Prin started to cry. Shawnese tried to console her while also trying to keep Jonah's head calm all the while freaking out herself.

The three waited as close to the forest as they were allowed, but the night started to fall and there was still no Amelia.

When Amelia had escaped the village, she felt a sense of liberation. 'I'll just go on a quick hike, just one or two miles, and then I'll come back,' she promised.

Amelia walked slowly through the vines and trees. There was so much shade, Amelia was sure there'd be little difference between day or night in some areas. Amelia found a cave and explored it for about twenty feet before it looked too far deep to continue any further. Having no one around felt exhilarating. "Hello," she cried up to the trees. She heard scurrying and distant calling of animals. 'Shawnese would love this,' she thought. There may not be any people, but the forest was littered in creatures. She heard a sort of cricking. When she looked up, she noticed it was a bird making the noise. 'I bet Prin would love to know what that bird is,' she thought. 'If she doesn't know it already.'

Everywhere she went, she could feel the purity of the forest. There was no sound of cars moving on roads, there were no distant house lights, there was no private property. Amelia rested by a creek and took out some food to munch on for a bit. She wondered if she should go back. Her running off probably worried her friends. "Just a couple hours," she said to herself. The sound of her voice always seemed to startle something nearby, which was somewhat satisfying to hear whatever it was scurrying away.

She wandered farther in and took note of a plant with purple leaves. It branched off of the ground like vines on the floor, and the center were five stocks growing together and twisting around each other in an explosion of more vines and leaves, but they became pink as they got to the top. "Wow," she breathed. With her desire to be as lack for technology as she could she didn't bring her phone or camera, but she wished she had then. 'Prin would flip if she saw this,' Amelia thought.

Amelia noticed a little while longer that she couldn't see very well anymore. She felt a rise in her chest. "Uh-oh," she muttered. "I really better get back now or I'm going to end up in a lot of trouble." She didn't think she had even been hiking that long. She tried to find her way back to the purple plant, which had become a landmark in her mind. She struggled to see her compass, turned in the right direction, and started going onward.

"I should have hit it by now," she muttered, gasping at the creatures that fled at the sound of her voice. There were less animal sounds now. Things were getting really quiet. Amelia wondered were the cicadas were now, and why they weren't singing anymore. Amelia stopped to take a flashlight out of her backpack.

"Rrrch!"

Amelia jumped and held the flashlight close to her, trying to make out in the darkness what she just heard was.

"Rrrch rrrch!"

Amelia quickly zipped up her pack and lit the flashlight on. Normally, she knew it was best to make a lot of noise in the forest to alert bears that would then stay away from the sound of the person. Amelia didn't know anything about these animals, so didn't know what the best decision would be about them.

Would she have to spend the night here? She didn't pack for that. Amelia turned on the flashlight and tried to calm herself down. "Okay Amelia come on, you got this. You just have to find some shelter and sleep it out for the night."

"Crit crit crit."

"What was that?!" Amelia spun wildly, trying to find what was making noises. She thought she saw a pair of nocturnal eyes in the darkness, but as she turned her flashlight to it there was nothing there.

"Oh please, please," Amelia whispered. "I'm sorry, I just wanted to get away from civilization for a little while, I don't want to die out here."

She warned herself to calm down. She had to keep positive. She had to tell herself that one night was no big deal. It was just like camping. "Just like with my family when I was younger," she reminded herself. She closed her eyes and slowed her breathing. She thought back about the camping trips with her family. She remembered fishing with her dad and playing UNO in the campsite with her mom and older sister. She remembered catching lizards and minnows in the water with her brother. She felt herself sigh in nostalgia.

"Mwwwoooorrrrrrrrrr!"

Amelia opened her eyes and spun the flashlight around. She could have sworn the sound came from right behind her.

She found herself at the mouth of a small cave. The wall of rocks startled her, but she looked into the cave warily and realized it was only about ten feet deep. She checked every crack and underneath rocks, but there was nothing in this cave. She hurried to bring her things inside and put her back to the wall. She felt much better now that she had shelter. In the darkness, she felt less a part of nature and much more like she was being hunted by it. But in the cave, she felt shelter. She couldn't help but cry thinking about how worried her friends must be. She thought about the legend of people being lost in the forest forever. No, she couldn't think like that. She closed her eyes and revisited her memories camping with her family and hiking with her friends. She always fantasized that she could survive the forest alone. After all, she felt so at peace with nature when she was hiking. Even when she traveled in the darkness with Prin, they had the stars and they had each other. Being in the forest this way, she didn't realize how terrifying it was being alone at night.

The next morning, she opened her eyes slowly. Once they were opened, she became aware of something moving around her. Amelia's body tensed. She was no longer in the cave. Whatever was moving around her was big. She tried very slowly to turn behind her and look.

It had antlers that grew up in elaborate swirls, and the head and body looked like a deer. It had four eyes and four ears underneath the antlers. The creature was as big as a Clydesdale, and it had something in its mouth. Amelia thought at first glance that it could be a large rabbit, but she was more focused on the deer-creature's huge fangs, like a saber-toothed tiger.

The deer turned its face right at Amelia. She froze, thinking this could be it. The deer's left ears twitched and rotated before the deer turned around and started bounding away, it's deer-like tail disappearing in the thicket of the forest.

Amelia felt as though she could breathe again. She sat up to notice that she was nowhere near any caves or cliff walls. In fact, nothing looked familiar at all. She looked around for her things and noticed her backpack hanging on the branch of a tree. Amelia jumped to knock her backpack down, and she caught it. "How did I get here?" She mumbled. How far was she from the village? She went into her backpack to take out her compass.

"Where is it?" she cried aloud. "My compass, where is it? Oh no," she emptied the backpack of the contents and there was no compass.

"The sun," she sighed. "I'll just climb one of these trees and try to find out where the sun is rising." She might even be able to see the village from that high up. Amelia sighed and put her backpack on, not wanting anything else to go missing. Amelia started climbing a tree with low branches, and tried to get herself all the way to the top.

Some branches were far apart so she had to take a few leaps. She didn't want to think about how much harder it would be to get down. Well, potentially it won't be hard at all, but terribly painful.

The leaves were bigger than the palm of her hand, and they intertwined together so much that breaching through the leaves was almost like opening a heavy door. She kept climbing, desperate to reach the top. "Come on, let me through," she grunted.

She breached the leaves, and she felt a chill and a huge gust of wind. It surprised her, since the ground was so peaceful without any sign of wind at all. She tried to find the source of the sun, but as soon as she began to absorb the sight of the sky, she felt herself start to cry.

It was daylight, but the sun was strangely missing. Worse yet, it was as though she were in the middle of an ocean of leaves. Every direction, every horizon looked exactly the same. There was no distinguishing feature, no source of light, and no sign of civilization anywhere.

"No, noooo," she cried. Where was the village, where were her friends? She was completely lost. There was no way out, she was lost forever.

Amelia started to climb down from the tree. On her way down, she saw something moving. Amelia paused to see what it was. She saw the side of it as it passed from one tree to the next not far from her. It was a giant spider, green and brown and almost perfectly camouflaged. It was the size of a cat.

"Oh no," she moaned, and almost lost her grip on the branch. She kept climbing down, spotting more of the spiders. "Aaah," she went to grab a branch, but it turned out to be one of the spider's legs. The spider jerked her away, hissed and ran off. It startled her, and she fell.

She screamed on her way down, but as she fell, she noticed somewhat that she didn't hit any branches. She kept falling when she thought she should have hit the ground by then. She was going to die, this was it.

She stopped falling, but she didn't hit anything. She opened her eyes and stopped screaming, and tried to reach for a ground. She twisted her body to look behind her, hoping to see some sort of safe ground or anything like that. There was the bed of leaves. She reached for it, unsure of why she was suspended in midair. Then, as though a cord had snapped, she fell on the bed of leaves.

"Okay, okay," she wiped her eyes and sniffed. "I get it, I understand. I shouldn't have run into the sacred woods. I just wanted to feel part of nature. Please, I just want to go home. Isn't there anything in this forest that will help me get back home?"

Silence was all that replied to her. She took a moment to cry, wiping her tears and trying to calm down. She picked herself up from the floor, and choosing a direction, started to head that way.

Amelia kept herself aware of the creatures in the forest. Now that she was aware these creatures were nothing like the ones she had ever seen, she had to be careful to not antagonize anything. She thought of what the guide said about the forest changing to confuse people. If that was the case, then the landmarks she had in her mind were no help to her. She hoped she could, at least, find a stream. Her water bottle was empty, and she was so thirsty. It occurred to her that she didn't seem in any danger, nothing had attacked her and even the nature itself seemed to have stopped her fall before. But she was scared, thinking that she may be lost forever if she didn't find some way to get out.

She thought about her friends. She hoped they didn't try to hunt for her in the forest. What if they were also lost in the forest? "If my friends are in here," Amelia begged the forest. "Please don't let them get lost because of me."

A bright, unnatural light beamed from the distance. It was as white as heaven's door. 'Or a flashlight,' she added in her mind hopefully. She hurried towards the light, not saying a word in case it was a sort of creature. The light started to dim, and Amelia started to run faster. Wait, don't go, she wanted to call out. But she didn't. By the time she got to the source, the light was very dim. It was coming from a tree.

The illuminating, white source was a face, poking out of the tree. The face looked serene and otherworldly. Her mouth was open wide, but her eyes were closed as though she was asleep. Around her, silver hair like strands of fine metal fell down the tree trunk, their individual strands flowing finely as a spider's thread.

Amelia became entranced. It was strange and gruesome, but somehow serene. It was something beautiful. She worried that saying anything would made the vision fade away. She took a step away from the tree she used as a hiding spot.

The ghoulish, yet strangely relaxing white-faced figure didn't move, but her hair started growing. It fell and twisted through the forest as though the face were the source of a stream of chrome. Amelia looked down to where the hair was growing. She recalled for a moment the story they were told in the village about a river of silver.

The hope in Amelia's chest rose again. Was this the silver river? Would this be the way home, or was it a trick? She had no other choice.

Amelia took one more look towards the glowing face, mouth agape, eyes daintily closed. She looked back down to the stream of hair.

She began to follow the path, but didn't dare say a word. She started out jogging through the forest. As the forest became denser, she had to slow down. She noticed then how the stream of hair also emitted a light glow. Small puffs of light drifted away from the hair, like embers in a heavenly fire. She walked beside it, keeping her eyes on possibly dangerous beings. She noticed, as the forest became dark as night, there were lights in the trees. The trees ceased and Amelia found herself going through a tunnel of vines through a cliff. On the walls were glowing blue mushrooms, like the lights that were on the branches of the trees before she entered the tunnel. The glow of the mushrooms caught minerals in the rock of the tunnel that shone like stars.

Amelia's breath caught in her throat. For a moment, she had forgotten her fear. It was one of the most beautiful things she had ever seen.

It was almost with regret that she passed through the tunnel to the other side. She tried to keep the memory of the tunnel in her mind, closing her eyes so that she could keep it. She wanted her friends to know about it, if she ever saw them again.

Amelia felt her legs ache. She stepped to the side to sit on a rock and eat what she had left of her snacks. As she ate, she noticed a faint sound in the distance. She crammed the last of her granola into her mouth and hurried to where she heard the noise.

It was the stream of water she had passed yesterday. She swallowed the granola and cupped her hands, enjoying the clear, cool feeling of the water. She took a drink. It was, to Amelia's mind, the perfect definition of refreshing. The water tasted like a breath of fresh air, as though she had been before holding her breath her whole life. She drank some more, but when she tried to fill her water bottle, the water went right through it as though it didn't exist at all. If she hadn't dealt with stranger things before, she might have been concerned. For now, she was only glad the water was there. It didn't necessarily mean she was going the right way, but it felt good to finally see something familiar.

She continued to follow the silver stream, her hopes raised and her walk determined. She stopped when she saw something off in a clearing. She hid behind a tree and took a look at what was moving around. Hopping around in the clearing were creatures that looked like neon blue, pink, purple and green rabbits. They had long ears, but they were longer than a normal rabbit. Their tails were longer and swayed like cat tails. They had long whiskers and bright brown eyes. They made a soft 'meep' noise as they hopped around grazing the grass, their little bodies moved every time they cried 'meep.' They seemed to put their whole bodies into making the noise, but it was so quiet regardless.

Amelia mused how Shawnese would adore these animals. She wondered if they were the creature the deer she saw before had in its mouth, and if Shawnese would want to keep or hunt it. Amelia took a bit of time watching these adorable creatures hopping around. She lost track of time for a moment. She lost track of urgency. She almost lost track of what she was doing before. The little neon rabbits started hopping away, and Amelia thought to follow them. "Wait," She whispered to herself. "Don't stray from the silver path. You want to go home Amelia, remember?"

Going back to the path, she caught sight of the purple plant she had seen. It took a lot to keep her from exclaiming with joy. That was two out of the three landmarks she had on her way in. She became determined to keep on the path, walking fast again, trying to keep her eye out for the cave she saw.

It was starting to get dark again. However, she was no longer afraid. On this guide back, knowing there was a way home, she felt her connection with nature again. Even as she traveled in the darkness, the dense forest started to ebb, and she was able to see the stars in the sky. They were so numerous Amelia was sure they would fall on her like glitter. The silver hair's glow was dimmer than Amelia remembered, but as long as she could still see it, she didn't pay much attention.

During her walk, she almost felt sad to leave the Lost Forest. It was filled with so many beautiful things, and since it constantly changed, she would never get bored hiking it. Honestly, it was everything she ever dreamed of. Maybe she could come back sometime. Or even, maybe just stay one more night.

Amelia stopped walking. She could see the edge of the forest now. Looking down, the silver stream of hair was gone. Amelia opened her mouth. "I could stay," she hadn't heard her voice in so long, it was louder than the forest, and it startled her. She could stay. Things were frightening, but she seemed to never be in any real danger. The forest was beautiful, and mystical, and there was nothing else like it in the world.

Amelia took a step back into the forest. "It's everything I wanted." Amelia felt pain similar to homesickness at the thought of leaving the forest.

Her legs mechanically took step after step, further into the woods. She could find the silver river again. She could stay just a little longer. The mushrooms, the interesting plants, the strange creatures, the night brimming with glittering stars, would she regret leaving it all behind? There might be more things yet unexplored. She took a few more steps into the forest.

Before the sight of the village faded completely, Amelia stopped before the silhouette of a large deer, antlers twirled, standing alert, welcoming. It waited for her. Her head bowed. "Thank you," she whispered. There was a moment of stillness before the deer bowed its head in return. For that moment, they both knew. They understood each other, and Amelia left a bit of her soul in the forest to remember her by. With the final blessing, Amelia turned and ran out of the forest. She wanted to stay, and felt as though she needed to stay, but her family was waiting for her. Her friends were waiting for her. She could hear her friends begging for her to return. Their voices were crisp in her mind, as though they were there with her.

"Her praying worked for you," Jonah asked their guide. They had remained in the guide's hut as guests, waiting for the return of their friend.

"My wife," the guide gestured to the old woman cooking. "Pray every night that I return. I hear her call and silver river bring me home."

Prin had her hands folded, staying silent, muttering her pleas to anyone who would listen to help Amelia find her way back.

"It's been so long now," Jonah whispered. "I'm all prayed out. What if she doesn't come back?"

"Don't say that," Shawnese called from the kitchen as she helped the guide's wife and daughter with the cooking. "Keep praying Jonah or I swear you'll wish you were lost in the woods."

Jonah sighed. "It'd be better to just go out and find her."

"No good," The guide replied. "You get lost too. Best stay here where she know you waiting."

"This is impossible, we should be filing a missing person's report or setting up a search party or something."

"Jonah, please," Prin told him. "I'm trying to pray."

Jonah looked over to Prin, fresh tears in her eyes. She had been crying for every day Amelia's been missing. He sighed and closed his eyes. He prayed with her. He prayed for Amelia to come back for all of them.

Moments later, there was commotion outside. Prin gasped and looked out the window again. Her heart nearly leapt out of her. "It's her! She's back!" Prin lept from her spot and sped out of the hut.

Shawnese and Jonas followed Prin outside, cheering and crying for Amelia's safe return. They embraced her. The embrace snapped Amelia out of her daze. "Guys?" she asked, hugging them back. Her disappearance came back to her quickly and she hugged her friends harder. "I'm so sorry I worried you, I didn't mean to be gone so long, I intended to only stay a few hours. I didn't know I would get lost until the next day."

"The next day," Prin wailed through her tears. "Amelia you were gone for five days!"

"How did you get back?" Shawnese demanded.

"It was," Amelia thought a moment. "A face in a tree. Her hair flowed down and showed me the way, like a stream of silver liquid."

"Are you sure you're okay, Amelia? You didn't eat anything weird, did you?"

"No, I didn't eat anything weird," Amelia replied. "Oh, but I saw something weird. And I have a lot of things to tell you guys about."

CHASING NIGHTMARES

The worst kind of dreams, Leonard would argue, are the ones where you are being chased by someone or something and you can't get away from them. Unfortunately, these were the sort of dreams that were common for Leonard. He didn't have them every night, but they were a few different nights where Leonard would experience the worst sort of dreams.

Leonard had an exceptionally sensitive reaction to light and sound. The smallest blinking light or the softest noise, when it was a bad day, could give him migraines. Sometimes, when he's having the worst time of his sensory sensitivity, even his dreams could be too loud or too bright.

There are creatures that roam nightmares. These demons act as symbols, or that's what some scholars believe. Leonard's dream, so vivid and full of demons, convinced him of these creatures. How else would these creatures have been made? Surely, he hadn't thought of them. They didn't resemble any movie or game he had ever played.

He dreads sleeping most nights. He knows they wait for him within his own mind. They lurk in his subconscious; a place where he has no control. It is the land in his own self that he cannot fully control. He remembered the first dream, being chased by the creatures made of darkness or perhaps black ink, smooth as oil and dripping like paint. The Fence was the first demon, beginning his torment with the screeching sound of metal against metal. He stood in a labyrinth of a house which had no exit, and he ran away from the sound. The metal screeching and moaning made his entire body tremble. He hoped that he could escape, knowing somehow that there would be none. He found himself in a dead end, and when he turned, he saw it.

The creature loomed over him, its head and eyes lowered at the sight of him, its target. Leonard became paralyzed, but he forced his body through the great creature, its limbs long and loud, twisting and swirling like an adorned porch beam. He kept running. He had to run.

The large, screeching creature gained its target and tried to swipe at him, but Leonard was able to duck away from it. The fence's eyes burned with unexpected rage toward Leonard, though

Leonard kept running. But the shrill noise deafened him, he was sure he would go mad from it.

He woke up, his heart pounding. His ears were ringing. The bedroom was suddenly so silent.

Leonard, interested in how or why he would experience such a dream, reverted to the unsteady science of it. Even in the psychological science of dreams, Leonard couldn't find much in the realm of deafening dreams being chased by demons. The problem became even more complicated at the introduction of 'bright-eyes Anubis.'

A figure, dark as tar and with the head of a dog, this man had big white round eyes that were as glaringly bright as headlights. Leonard tried to run, as he always does, but he had found himself too terrified to walk. Throughout the dream, he was unable to run. Instead, he would have to hide from the dangers of the 'Bright-Eyed Anubis' which stalked places near him, his eyes like blinding spotlights. When he woke up, he would try to stand and his legs would feel unsteady.

The dog-headed man's eyes were so bright that it petrified Leonard. He had to be silent, he had to stay in the darkness. Leonard shied under tables and around corners where the blinding light couldn't reach him. Once the Dog-headed man spotted him, Leonard had to scramble back into the darkness. It seemed to confuse the creature and it would turn to continue its stalking.

These two terrors often kept Leonard from a good-night's sleep. Leonard tried to explain the dream to others, but no one seemed to understand what he meant. Leonard was in high school, and though making friends for him was easier than when he was younger, he didn't have anyone that he felt he could trust such an intimate thing as dreams to them. He finally confided in his older brother, Lyle. Leonardo waited at the door frame of his brother's room.

Lyle took a passing glance at his brother. "What's up, nerd?" he asked before going back to playing his MMO.

Leonard considered going back to his room and forgetting about asking his brother for help. What made him think this would be a good idea?

"You gonna stand there all day or are you gonna tell me what's up?"

"Um, uh," Leonard took an inch closer, but he wasn't sure if he was allowed to enter his brother's room without direct permission. "I was hoping we could talk?"

"We are talking-oh you sack of shit I'm coming for you just you wait!"

Leonard jumped.

"Sorry bro, just talking to the game."

Leonard wanted to ask Lyle to pause the game, or tell his friends he'd be back. Leonard felt uncomfortable talking about something as intimate as feelings in such an un-intimate way. "Nothing, sorry," Leonard turned to leave. He didn't want to bother his brother, maybe another time.

Lyle had a hard time reading his brother sometimes. He was so timid, yet he seemed uninterested in everything. Lyle knew it was just hard for Leonardo to express how he felt or understand others, but sometimes it felt like he was doing it on purpose. At that moment, for instance, Leonard walks up to Lyle's door frame, doesn't say anything and nearly gave Lyle a heart attack having suddenly showed up there. Lyle was the first one to have to speak to hide the thrill he felt in his chest when he suddenly saw Leo there. Lyle called out to him to relieve the tension he felt in the air, and his brother replies with a serious, almost angry tone. Now he didn't want to talk at all. Still, he grew up with Lyle long enough to know something was on his brother's mind. "Sorry guys, gimme a sec. I have to go do some stuff."

He left his game and walked over to Leonard's room. He knocked on the door, "Hey bro, can I come in?"

"Yeah," Leonard replied. He was sitting in the dark, on his bed. The light had been bothering him lately and needed a bit of time in the darkness. He turned his head to the door to see if Lyle would decide to come in.

When Lyle opened the door, he saw his brother staring at him in the darkness. He sat there, watching, like an ominous presence. Dang, why did his brother have to be so creepy?

"Hey Leo, mind if I turn on the light?"

"Yes. Sorry, my head hurts."

Lyle lowered his hand from the switch. "Not feeling well?"

"No, I'm fine," Leonard lied.

"So you wanted to talk to me?"

"No, it's nothing." Leonard didn't want to bother his brother. Besides, how could Lyle help?

Lyle felt tempted to leave. Leonard said he didn't want to talk, but Lyle felt compelled today to be a good brother. He could tell that Leonard wasn't too happy. It wasn't really in the way he moved and talked since Leonard always acted like this, but there was definitely something wrong. "Hey, I'm sorry if I upset you."

"You didn't upset me," Leonard replied. He was looking down, unable to meet his brother's eye. His eyes hurt too much, he had to close them. But he wasn't upset, that much was true. "Sorry I interrupted your game."

"Oh, that?" Lyle chuckled. "Don't worry about it, I can play with those losers any day. Come on bro, do you need to talk? I'm here for you, man."

Leonard sighed, "Just been having nightmares, lately." He had actually been having the nightmares for years. Researching dreams had become his hobby, it was practically all he talked about.

"Nightmares, huh? Like what kind of nightmares?" Lyle was a bit interested in that sort of stuff as well, but with Leonard so obsessed with it Lyle eventually started almost dreaded the topic. Leonard was too obsessed, he thought.

"A fence-looking shadow creature and a man with a dog's head and spotlight eyes," Leonard replied.

It took Lyle a second. "What kind of fence are we talking about? Chain-link, wooden?"

"No, like fancy metal swirls," Leonard tried to explain. "Kind of like the railing in front of our aunt's porch, you know? The metal swirls that look like hearts."

"Oh, you mean the 's' shaped things," Lyle nodded. "Okay, so that and a guy with a dog's head and... Spotlight eyes?"

"Really bright eyes that blare out and blind you," Leonard elaborated. Just thinking about it made his eyes hurt, and he covered his eyes with his hands for maximum darkness.

Lyle had a moment of sympathy for his brother. He always had such a hard time with light and sound. He remembered as a kid, when Leonard couldn't speak yet, nobody knew what was wrong. Leonard would throw fits, and being six, everyone would urge him to 'just tell them what was wrong.' No one knew how much pain Leonard was in. "Sounds like a rough time, Leo." He wished he knew what he could do to help. His brother was creepy at times, but he was still Lyle's little bro. "I don't know how to get rid of nightmares. If I did, I'd get rid of them for you."

"It's okay," Leonard lied. He didn't really know what he was expecting, either. What could his brother do to help him?

That night, Leonard fell asleep.

However, Leonard did not wake up.

"What's wrong with him?" Lyle could hear his father in hysterics while his mother tried to calmly figure out what happened. Lyle was just waking up, so he wasn't sure what was happening.

He walked out of his room, groaning and tired. His father hurried up to him with such fret that Lyle thought he'd hit him although their father never hit anyone in his life.

"What do you know about this?" His father demanded.

"About what?" Lyle asked, walking with his father into his brother Leonard's room. Leonard looked as though he were fast asleep. Lyle didn't understand. "Leo's just asleep."

"No," his mother corrected, "We've tried waking him up for school and he won't wake up."

"Maybe he's just fooling around," Lyle offered. He walked up to Leonard as the parents argued over what could be happening to their youngest son. "Hey, Leo. You gonna wake up for our parents or what? Come on man, don't freak them out like this." There was no response. "Here I come to tickle you," Lyle grinned, and tickled Leo's side, but still nothing. Lyle tried to get his brother to smile, or push him away, or call out to him, or anything. But no matter what he did, Leonard wasn't waking up.

The hospital came to take him in. Leonard was in a coma for an unknown cause. It became a devastating reality for Leonard's family, especially Lyle who was the last to talk to his brother.

Lyle thought about that conversation as though it would provide his with some sort of clue. The dreams that his brother was so obsessed with, it was such a regular conversation for Leonard, Lyle didn't think much on it at the time. Lyle wondered if people dreamed in comas, and if so, what about? Was Leonard facing those chasing demons in his dream right now? No, no that's not something to be thinking about. Still, now that it was in Lyle's mind, he couldn't help but think about it. It couldn't just be coincidence that it was the last thing Leonard mentioned before passing out.

Was his brother in a never-ending perpetual nightmare with the two demons Leonard was talking about? Lyle didn't like the thought of his brother suffering. Creepy or not, he was still Lyle's little brother.

Lyle went into Leo's room to try and figure out some clues. No one had ever really invaded Leonard's space before, so now that they were all easy to access, Lyle could see all of the research and documents and journal entries his brother kept. Lyle's heart stung. According to his journals, Leonard had been suffering from these chasing nightmares ever since the two of them were very young.

Leonard had been in a coma for nearly two weeks. Whenever Lyle wasn't at work, he was in Leonard's room trying to read through all of his brother's dream information. He couldn't manage to play games with his friends while his brother was facing the demons on his own. Lyle started having dreams about these demons himself. He dreamed that Leonard was running away from two ghastly creatures. He cried out to Leonard, but his voice couldn't be heard over the loud screeching of the metallic monster. The Anubis-like creature caused Lyle's chest to freeze in fear as well, but he wasn't their target. The nightmares left Lyle hopeless for his brother.

At last, there came a moment of realization. In the notes, one professor claimed that dreams were solely created with memory. Memory was most often triggered by smell.

Lyle took the afternoon off work to drive to the hospital where Leo was staying. He brought a bunch of smelly things in a duffel bag. "Leo, don't worry. I'm going to get you out of that coma…" Lyle put a hand on his brother's wrist. After a moment, Lyle took out one of their mother's scented candles which she kept everywhere in the house. He couldn't light it up in the room, but he placed it by his brother's nose and hoped it would do something. "Come back to me, bro. Come on, Leo. Please hear me."

Nothing happened on the first day, but Lyle was not about to give up. Every day, he came to visit Leo for a few hours carrying familiar things. He used fresh sheets, bananas which were always in the kitchen, even one of Lyle's dirty socks. It had been nearly five days, and there had been no response.

Lyle, desperate, brought back the scented candle again. He placed it in the hospital room and lit it, and held his brother's hand. He could get kicked out doing this, but he had to do something. He needed his brother back. Lyle had closed the curtains, closed the door and turned off the lights. "Nice and dark and quiet, just as you like," Lyle whispered.

From then on, Lyle didn't say a word. He just sat next to his brother, holding his hand, waiting.

Lyle had fallen asleep beside Leonardo's bed. Shapes and colors swirled within his mind, and within the ether, he heard a familiar voice.

"Lyle, you're here?"

Lyle turned his head. In an instant, the realm he entered came into focus. Beside him was his brother, Leo, awake and talking.

"Leo thank Almighty, I'm so glad to see you," He went to hug his brother, but stopped short at the sudden flash of a white light. His heart skipped a beat as he saw the lights shaking, something running almost impossibly fast towards them. Lyle took Leo's arm and helped him crawl under a flight of stairs that stood as a porch to a house that seemed strikingly similar to their aunt's. "Quick," Lyle whispered. "We'll go in here."

"Wait," Leonard clung to his brother's shirt. "That's where the Fence lives."

Lyle turned to look at his brother. Leonard wasn't his usual hard-to-read self. In this place, at this moment, Lyle could see horror in his little brother's eyes, and fear shook his little brother's voice.

It stirred something within Lyle. He felt angry. He sought vengeance. "Don't worry, Leo. I'm here now, I got your back."

Despite Leonard's quiet objections, Lyle made his way up the porch steps and into the building with his mortified sibling in tow. The instant they passed through the door, their entrance faded from sight. They were among pointless stairwells and rooms and floors. "What is this, an abstract painting?" Lyle questioned. Leonard clutched his brother's arm. "We shouldn't be here, Lyle."

The rapid screeching that followed was so shrill that it made Lyle's teeth hurt. "Follow me," He shouted. Even as he moved and yelled for his brother to follow, all he could hear was the screeching. It came from everywhere. The house itself was screaming. Lyle halted at the sight of black transparent tar oozing from the hole above them. It lowered itself like a Goliath, a man form completely comprised of screeching, swirling steel. Its white eyes and gaping mouth matched Lyle's scream. He turned towards Leo and they fled together. It was so hard to think, the screeching was consistent, annoying, terrifying. This was what plagued his brother's mind at night?

They found themselves out of the house, in a yard surrounded by a picket fence to the clouds idly drifting above them. Waiting for them at the edge of the yard was the dog-headed man, his eyes shining straight at the two boys.

Lyle felt practically blind by the lights. The creature made his way forward. Lyle's legs wouldn't move. He saw Leonard fall to his knees. "Leo," Lyle tried to cry out. His brother's eyes were wet with tears, his previously expressive face drained to the indifferent stare that Lyle was familiar with. The noises, the lights, that's when Lyle realized it. It was just too much for Leonard's brain to process. He was shutting down.

Lyle dropped to his knees before Leonard, the creatures closing in. Lyle felt his ears hurt. He was sure they'd start bleeding. His eyes stung so much he could see only blurry shapes. The creatures were closing in.

He searched for Leonardo's shoulders and embraced his brother. He shielded the light from Leo with his chest and put his hands over his little brother's ears. He couldn't hear himself saying it, but he kept whispering 'sshhhh, it's okay. Don't focus on the noise. Sssshhhh.'

The incessant screeching gave way to beeping, which woke Lyle up. Groggily, he moaned and yawned. It wasn't until he noticed what the noise was that he woke up suddenly. The heart monitor, it was picking up its pace!

Lyle kept quiet, waiting. He squeezed his brother's hand. "Leo, can you hear me bro? Come back bro, come on."

"Lyle?" Leonard's weak voice called out. "Lyle."

"Yeah bro, it's me," Lyle was so happy, he started to fight back tears. "How are you feeling, bro?"

"The nightmares," he mumbled. "How long was I asleep?"

"Few weeks now, pal?"

Leonard was silent a moment and looked to his brother as though he didn't believe him. "What about school?"

Don't worry about that now Leo, jeez. You just got out of a coma!" Lyle told him. He hurried to blow out the candle before he got caught. They must have not been out for long, though it felt like a hundred hours. "So what about those nightmares?"

Leonard turned his head to the drawn curtains. He then turned his head to the candle which was halfway burned. At last, his eyes shifted to Lyle, and he smiled. "You made them quiet."

THEY WATCH STILL

I hope that you remember me. It has been a while since I've been able to write to you and I must apologize, I have to make it as brief as I can. I fear that I may have gone too far.

It's very tempting to look at them. But you cannot look. You must not look. I know they are staring at me, but as I become more secluded, the less they seem to hide their presence from me. I feel as though it's a challenge. Whatever it is, whoever 'they' are, they know I'm trying to unravel their mystery. They know that I'm trying to learn their mystery.

As long as I'm with other people, they don't appear. When I am with other people, shadows remain shadows. I am currently writing this letter while at a party. There is a lot of noise and it's hard to focus, but it's safer than being alone. There's something I must do. I have managed to gain an interview with someone. It's the wife from the psychiatrist which died in the woods. 'He was so healthy. So stable and healthy,' she said to me. She had said it many times, in fact. It's been fifteen years since the tragic event happened, yet her eyes were fresh with sorrow.

I asked her to tell me what her husband said before he left. She said 'the usual things. He would talk about his plans and how some fresh mountain air would do him good. It was strange for him to take a vacation, but he seemed so sure it was going to help.' She looked down at her drink. I had asked her out to a local coffee shop so we could talk. 'There was something he kept doing though,' she confessed. 'His eyes kept shifting to the side. After I saw the,' she paused, her chest heaving. 'After I saw the journal, I realized he kept looking over to his shadow.'

Her eyes turned toward me, begging for answers. 'He knew more about the human psyche than anything. He can determine truth from hallucinations. He should have been immune, shouldn't he? No trauma, no human history had ever occurred to make him act like he did. I thought I knew him, but,' her mouth went to her hand and she closed her eyes. I remained silent, giving her quiet praise and hoping she would continue.

When it was clear she had finished, I asked another question. "Why didn't you go with him on the vacation?"

'I had to work. I've given the police my alibi already, it's confirmed with my time cards.' She took a drink from her hot tea, her hands shaking slightly. 'He said he needed time alone anyway, so he could think. He told me there was nothing to worry about.'

I drank my coffee for a pause, but she was the first to speak up before I had the chance to. 'What did you say you were researching again?' I told her it was just a personal sort of research concerning similar hallucinations. 'Have you seen the hallucinations before?' I told her I had not. 'If you find what it takes to see such hallucinations, please let me know.'

The cabin the psychiatrist had stayed in still belonged to her. I asked if I could take a look. Since police took all that they cared to find, it was no longer under investigation. She agreed to let me into her property, so there I went into the last place the psychiatrist was ever known to be alive.

All the window shades were drawn. I turned the light on inside to a nice two-bedroom log-cabin. I noticed how barren it looked, for a place that was supposed to be like a getaway. I reminded myself that a bunch of things might have been confiscated. I didn't know what I expected to find in the house, but I was desperate to find anything new. This psychiatrist had an experience with the shadow-eyes that nobody else had. He had done some research on them, and I was sure that he had to have gathered information and I only hoped the police hadn't managed to gather all of it.

All the mirrors were gone. I hadn't realized it until I went into the bathroom and the medicine cabinet door was missing. There were places on the walls where obvious things were hanged. Some full-body mirrors that were in the two bedrooms were built into the building, and all that was left of them were the mirror frames. I tried to imagine what had happened to them. Did the psychiatrist take them out himself? Were they confiscated for evidence? If they were confiscated, why would they be considered proof? What was on them? If they had not been confiscated, where were they now?

The cabin itself was a spacious, toasty place. I marveled at the carved wood and stone. The kitchen looked brand new. The cabin was like a little paradise, so why is it that the psychiatrist couldn't relax in this place? I saw something move at the corner of my eye, in my shadow. I didn't dare look towards it.

There were lights everywhere. Every wall socket had a light of some sort hooked up to it. I wondered if maybe the psychiatrist tried at one point to drown out the shadow. I wonder how well that worked out.

After finding little to go on, I sat on the living room couch to rest. I heard a light crinkling, and I froze. I bounced a little on the cushion, and heard the crinkling again. There was something under the couch.

Eagerly, I thrust my hand into the plush treasure chest and was rewarded for my efforts. In my hand was a stack of notes from the Psychiatrist. I hurried to look at them, but was immediately let down by his atrocious penmanship. It would take some careful reading for it. It's so bad it'll be like deciphering a code.

I left them at my home, but since I've been at the house the eyes have been much more restless. That is why I'm here, in a party, writing this. I haven't had time to decipher, I've been too afraid to be alone. I hope it sounds like a reasonable fear. The eyes developed a routine where they show up all the time when I'm alone.

I will try to decipher the notes by the next time I write. Until then, don't lose hope.

THE SCARECROW AND THE LADY IN BLUE

Grace had moved into the old house not too long ago. It was truly by the good heart of a kindly elderly couple that she was able to find a place to stay. Ever since she was very young, she wanted to get into entertainment, but it was hard to do without parental support. While she was half a continent away, she hoped her family would at least show a bit of pride for her, trying so hard to fulfill her dreams, but they didn't even call on Holidays or send gifts or good wishes on her birthday anymore.

She moved to this big city with some cash in her pocket, a promised job, and a stable room-mate. Instead what she had was a flaky person who acted more like a pet and less like a responsible adult, and a promised job which was promised to someone else. Grace was resource-less, job-less, and homeless.

The grandparents of Grace's friend back home happened to live in the next town. They didn't even know Grace, but they offered for her to stay with them in their house until she was stable enough to get her own place. Grace accepted wholeheartedly and got her happy butt to a taxi. She settled into the elderly couple's empty bedroom which had their last child just move out of. Grace understood this may be due to a little bit of empty nest syndrome, but Grace was happy to take it for the way it is. Empty Nest or not, it was a nest. For Grace, it was more than she had before.

Grace was living there rent-free, so she developed a habit of doing the dishes while she was there. She went out looking for jobs, and in her spare time she tried out auditions for stand-up comedy. She had taken improvisation classes in school and felt as though she had a good performance, but she needed to be better. There were people who were so good at their comedy she would watch and find herself laughing hysterically.

Grace found a job across the street from a well-known theater. Her work was at a small convenience store, but at least they paid Grace with money and did so on time. She used it for food, which she got at a discount at the convenience store, a little bit for the elderly couple, and the rest she used to keep going for all the auditions.

Grace came home and waved to the old woman. "Good afternoon," Grace chimed.

"Hello Grace," the old lady called. "Any luck on those auditions yet?"

It was a question the old lady asked every day. It was odd but nice to have someone who cared. "Not yet, ma'am, but I'm crossing my fingers." Grace turned down the hallway, but before she passed to her room she froze. Her attention turned to the painting in the hallway. She noticed something that she didn't think she ever noticed before.

To be fair, Grace only looked at the paintings in passing. This one was the image of a young woman in a blue dress, holding a matching parasol as she stood in the middle of a wheat field. Grace always noticed the lady in the picture was a little to the right which had her feeling the painting was off-center, but she wasn't about to trump artistic expression forms that others enjoyed. So what if the girl was a little to the right, it showed off the wheat more, the golden glean of wheat.

She never noticed, until now, that there was something else in the picture. In the distance, behind the woman, there was a boy. The boy, however, had much bigger blue eyes. They looked much more like button eyes, in fact. The boy wore a hat with blonde hair underneath. The hair looked straight and straw-like. Grace looked closer at the boy. She stared at his eyes and his posture. The boy was walking, but his features looked very similar to that of a scarecrow.

Grace wasn't normally freaked out by scarecrows. In this instance, however, when she had spent weeks living there and she just couldn't remember ever seeing the boy in the background, she couldn't help but feel a tad perturbed.

"Gorgeous, isn't it?"

Grace jumped, and then put her hand to her chest. "Ah, oh, I didn't expect you to follow me. Yeah, it's a nice picture."

"I won it at an art museum. They say the painter, Van Rickson, put a little bit of himself into every painting. They say he had a habit of making the paintings come to life."

"Yeah I can really see that dynamic with the scarecrow."

"Scarecrow?" The old lady looked at the picture, thought a moment, and said, "Huh. I don't remember him in the painting."

Thoroughly chilled, Grace said her good-byes and went into the bathroom to try and have a nice, relaxing shower. She calmed down, convincing herself that the old woman was forgetful in her age and the fact that she couldn't remember the scarecrow slowly walking up to the lady in the blue bonnet was completely normal; Just old age, nothing strange or sinister or creepy about that. Grace would have thought to ask the old lady to elaborate, but she was also just fine with assuming that it was all just forgetfulness. If she could spin it right, maybe she could make this whole experience a good routine for her stand-up comedy.

A couple more weeks passed, and Grace hadn't thought much more about the picture with the scarecrow in it. She was too busy trying to juggle her real-life issues. The moment arrived, at last, where she thought she could enter her big break. A producer from the theatre Grace worked across from often came into the store for a hot dog or vitamin water. Every so often, she would talk to the guy. He often told her that he thought she was funny, and she should do stand-up comedy.

He came in one day with a proposal. He said that he found a late-night club looking for a good act, and he suggested Grace's stand-up comedy. Grace was ecstatic. She agreed instantly, and she was walking on air the rest of the day. The performance was in a week and a half, so she had to be ready by then. The producer would be in the audience, so maybe if she could prove to him how well she did with the crowd, he'll be able to help her into more doors.

Grace couldn't wait to tell the elderly couple the good news. She got home as fast as she could and hurried inside. She saw the old man, first. "I got a gig set up," she told him, grin as wide as the crescent moon.

"That's great news! Make sure to read the fine print," the old man replied. "I remember once, when I was a bit older than you, I was going to be in a big shot play. I was excited that I would get to be in the play, so I failed to read the fine print."

Never mind the fact that by now everyone knew the dangers of not reading contracts, the old man had a tendency to ramble. She didn't want to be rude and admit that she had a lot to do to get her act ready. His stories were pretty interesting a lot of the time, but sometimes there wasn't really much to the story than 'be careful to do this, I didn't and it burned me later.' She had a skit impersonating the way he told his stories, too. She did her act for the couple before and they thought it was a hoot. They didn't seem to get that the old man's long stories and the old woman's forgetfulness were things that they actually did, or perhaps they just had a good sense of humor and recognized the flaws enough to laugh about them.

The man was nearing the end of his story when the wife walked in with food for the animals. "I got a gig," she told the woman excitedly.

"Congratulations, we knew you could do it," the old woman exclaimed. "When is the show? Manny and I will try to make it."

Grace told them the date of the show, then politely went to practice. She froze again, at the painting.

The scarecrow was right next to the lady with the bonnet.

"Hey Dinah? Is this the same picture we were talking about a few weeks back?"

"What picture?" Dinah asked, walking up with Manny in tow.

"You know, when we were talking about the art auction and you mentioned this painting and not remembering the scarecrow?"

"Hasn't it always been there?" Dinah puzzled. After a moment, she decided. "It must have been," the old lady waved her hand and dismissed the conversation, turning away.

"Wait, no, you said it wasn't there before."

"That painting," the old man started. "We got that painting thirty-three years ago at an art auction."

"Yes, Dinah and I-,"

"I wasn't finished," Manny interrupted. "It was painted by this fellow, very young at the time, his name was Van-something."

"Van Rickson, yeah, Dinah and-,"

"Right, Van Rickson. An odd thing about this man, he had a habit of making the pictures seem like they could come to life."

Grace, seeing the escape was futile, conceded. "Is that so?" She asked.

"Yeah, creepy stuff," the old man finished. He turned and started to walk away.

Relieved that he cut it short on his own, she retreated back into her room. She tried to work on her gig, but she kept thinking about the painting. "Van Rickson," she thought aloud.

Grace typed up his name on a search engine. There were some really gorgeous paintings that showed up on image search, but a lot of the paintings were dark and ominous. She felt uncomfortable looking at them. She looked for a biography. "Here it is," She muttered. She just wanted to know a little bit about him, then she would go back to her gig. Apparently, Van Rickson was a famous artist in the early 20th century. He was a recluse and some would say even mad. He married a woman named Angel who died in a sanitarium years later. Van Rickson himself died in his house from a strange fire. 'Even as Van Rickson's charred body was found, the remaining paintings in the building were untouched,' the article said.

Attached to the story was a tab for 'scary myths.' Curious, Grace clicked it. There was a new message about paintings attacking people in the past. The paintings, the page claimed, were all haunted with Van Rickson's restless soul. There was a creepy section where a witness talked about how she was almost lured in by a monster, and the only way the paintings ever let her be was after they'd been burned.

"Freaky," Grace muttered. She closed the story before she got too paranoid and tried to focus on her first gig.

The night of the gig had quickly approached. Grace was incredibly nervous and tried a few breathing exercises. She tried to think about the comedy and not of the picture of the scarecrow and the woman in the blue dress. She developed a habit of looking at it every day to see if anything had changed or not. If there were, they were so slight that Grace didn't notice. Still, she knew she wasn't crazy. That painting as something terrible, she knew it.

She was able to perform wonderfully. The whole audience ended up laughing a lot. Grace had forgotten about everything except for how excited she was that everything was working out. She spoke to the producer a while who asked her to come to the theatre after her shift the following Monday. She happily obliged.

"We'll be going out to dinner," Dinah went over to tell Grace. "Do you have your key in case you get home before us?"

"Yes ma'am," Grace replied. The elderly couple left, and shortly afterwards so did Grace. The house was dark and silent when she made it, so she was, in fact, the first to come home. She turned the key and opened the door. She turned on the light.

Standing in the corridor, there was a smiling, blue-eyed scarecrow, staring and standing limply before her.

Grace froze.

With a sudden dash, the scarecrow leaped at Grace. She screamed and grabbed an umbrella sitting next to the door. She whacked at him and caught him off-balance. Grace ran towards the hallway and looked at the picture.

The wheat was stained with red, and the lady in the blue dress was face-down in the wheat, everything she wore was stained red. "Oh my Almighty," Grace breathed.

The scarecrow ran after her again.

Grace ran into her room and closed and locked the door. She remembered the story she read before. "Match, match, match," she mumbled. Grace knew she had some sort of torch. Holding onto the picture with one arm, she ruffled through all her things to try and find something she could use.

The scarecrow slammed against the door, and Grace shrieked. She kept searching, begging to find anything useful. She bought a lighter she thought. It had to be somewhere.

'BANG!' went the door.

"Go away holy Hell!" Grace shrieked. After a few more seconds of running around looking for the lighter, she found it in yesterday's pants pockets. She flipped it up and turned towards the door, shaking violently, she unlocked it.

The scarecrow, smiling and staring with blue buttons, looked at Grace who had the lighter under the painting. "G-go one step clo-closer," she stuttered. "And I'll burn you to Hell!"

The scarecrow paused a second, then held out his arms and reached for her.

Grace hurriedly jumped out of the way and made sure the lighter would touch him. He burst with flame suddenly. Grace didn't think he would be that flammable, but once she lit the scarecrow on fire, he quickly turned to ashes.

Grace looked at the portrait in her arms, and stared dumbfounded. The woman in blue, once dead, was right where she was before. The scarecrow wasn't in the picture at all.

NIGHT RIDER

It's never a good thing to drive when you're dog tired. Rolf tried to do so several times, but like he and all natives of this town know, there is a curse against late-night tired drivers. Rolf recently spent extra hours to close up shop, so he was more tired than usual after work. He fumbled with his car keys, yawned, and managed to unlock the door. The drive wasn't too far, maybe six minutes. He knew about the rumors that there was a motorcyclist that would drive with his headlight blaring behind late night drivers, but Rolf didn't care much for the rumor and didn't take the rumor seriously. The town was huge and it was a slim chance that whoever the motorcyclist was would decide to go down this particular muddy back road behind the grocery store even if they did exist.

Rolf started his car, yawning again. "I'll listen to some music to keep me awake," he decided aloud. He was sure talking to himself accompanied with loud music should be more than enough to keep him awake for six more minutes.

Rolf pulled out of the driveway, and not a second too soon, a motorcyclist drove behind him. Rolf wasn't sure why anyone would be out riding at two in the morning, let alone around late winter. Even then, Rolf doubted that this motorcyclist was the same from the rumors. He drove on, giving it little thought.

The motorcyclist was driving pretty close to Rolf's bumper. His headlights were blaring, too. Rolf tried moving the rearview mirror in order to see better without the it reflecting the light in his eyes. He tried speeding up a bit, but the motorcyclist followed. Rolf went as fast as he felt comfortable and the motorcyclist still kept up. Rolf wasn't sure why, but he was starting to feel unsettled by the motorcyclist. Rolf started taking sporadic, winding turns but the motorcyclist kept up the pace. Rolf heightened the volume of the music. The motorcyclist's engine was too loud to ignore.

Rolf wound back to the street he needed to be on when it occurred to him that, if he were to go home now, this motorcyclist would follow him. They would know where he lived. Rolf tried to move the mirror to look at the motorcyclist's face, but it was obstructed from the blaring headlights. Rolf tried slowing down and moving to the right so the motorcyclist could pass. The motorcyclist did move in front of Rolf, but only to drive directly in front of him. Rolf tried to start going again, but as he drove home, he realized that the motorcyclist was also driving in the same direction as his house.

This filled Rolf with dread. He stopped the car. The motorcyclist stopped, too. Rolf started the car, and the motorcyclist started his motorcycle as well, going in the same direction.

"What is this guy?" He muttered to himself as he tried to understand what this guy wanted.

Rolf had an idea. As he drove home, there came a street where he would randomly take a turn. It would throw off the motorcycle person so that Rolf could quickly drive home in piece without the threat of the motorcyclist knowing where he lived. Rolf waited until the last block, and then took an immediate left instead of going straight. Triumphant, Rolf grinned and turned his head to look forward at the task again

"Whoa-," Rolf slowed his car immediately out of reflex. In front of him was the black-suited motorcyclist. "How did they," his voice trembled. The motorcyclist went straight. He saw it! Rolf stopped his car and went in reverse to go the right way home. There was the motorcyclist again, in front of Rolf's car.

It was the Night Rider, after all. Rolf's heart pounded fiercely with the force of a piston. He knew there was no way around it. He would have to drive home with the spirit motorcyclist, the Night Rider. Rolf never knew anyone who experienced the Night Rider in person, so he didn't know what would happen to him afterword. Even the stories about the Night Rider were cryptic, just talking about the phantom rider that would antagonize late-night drivers. Were they an actual phantom? Were they demon? Would they take his soul?

He parked his car home and he turned off the ignition. His ears rang with how silent everything suddenly became. He felt his skin crawl and chill. Rolf willed himself to be brave and look behind him.

The Night Rider was gone. Rolf shifted his body to see better. He scanned his yard with wide eyes, and he strained his ears for noises. He couldn't have imagined it. The motorcyclist was right behind him. He still remembered the revving of the engine and the sight of the dark figure speeding by. Even with all this fresh in his mind, the only thing Rolf could hear as he sat in his driveway was the persistent wind through the trees.

THE BLIND SPOT

It's a proven fact, thanks to neuroscience, that a person's eyes have a blind spot. When I was younger, I thought that there were people who lived in our eyes. You know when you see something in the corner of your eye and you look and they're not there? I thought that was the person living in your blind spot. I call 'em 'Shadow Chasers,' because you're literally chasing the shadows with your eyes.

I thought it was cool, but of course my mom had to tell me the hard facts. 'Olive,' she says. 'There is no way that you can have people living in your eye. It's impossible, not to mention,' yadda yadda. She never took me seriously, not for anything. Well fine, so I'll become a neuroscientist and prove her wrong.

So that's what got me into neuroscience, proving my mother wrong. I know she's right now, of course. I never told her she was right, that would make things harder for me to talk to her about other things. Don't worry, proving her wrong didn't become the only reason, or even the biggest reason that I started getting a degree for neuroscience in the end. Fascination played a bit part of it, and also my little sister having trouble with her nerve endings made me passionate about learning more so I could help her, and there was this girl I liked at the time I was applying for colleges who almost went to the same college I went to. Anyway, proving my mom wrong was not the only reason, but it was the first.

It might sound stupid, but every so often I kinda think about the little people in your blind spot. I know it's not really possible, but the mind trick is really interesting. Since your blind spot just fills in things that the rest of your input sees, it can get things wrong all the time. I even gave my shadow chaser a name; Mildred. Why not? I see her all the time. I know she's not real but why should that stop me from having a little fun with my own mental flaws?

This girl Laurissa is trying to get her degree in medicine. She knows a lot about this sort of stuff. She's really smart. Pretty too. Anyway, Laurissa and I were talking about sight and how it can be rendered pretty much useless with the right kind of technology. It was really wild how she knew about all this sort of stuff. She explained that she had a cousin that went blind and they were able to wire him up to be able to see with his tongue. His TONGUE. You can do that kind of stuff! The human body is wild. Technology is wild.

I asked her what she thought about Mildred.

"Who?" she asked.

"Mildred. Have I not talked about her before? She's the person I see out the corner of my eye before I turn around."

"You named it?" she asked.

"Why, is that weird?" I asked in return. She kinda just looked at me, and then snorted.

"Yes," she responded. "But that's alright, it's a cool kind of weird. Just don't tell me you talk to her."

"Um," I fell silent.

"You know, I never really met anyone like you, Olive. You're pretty unique."

My heart did a lot of flips and turns, but I had to be sure. "The good kind of unique?"

"Oh absolutely," she replied. My heart proceeded to flip and turn. "Also, by the sound of it, I don't think it happens to me as much as it does to you."

"What do you mean 'as much'?" I inquired.

"Well, how often do you see the… Mildred?" Laurissa tilted her head to the side a bit, something she does when she's curious. It's adorable when she does it, like a puppy hearing a high-pitched noise.

I shrugged, "I always see her," I confessed. "I thought everyone was like that, just that invisible person always out the corner of your eye except you know they're not there but you have to look anyway but you were right."

"Not everyone has had that happen to them," Laurissa informed me. "Even if they did, it wouldn't be for so long, and they would see the shadows on few occasions, usually through lack of sleep or something like that. I've never had a person tell me they see it ALL the time."

"I must be pretty special then, huh?" Though to be honest, it made my gears whirr. Could that mean that I have a symptom for something? What would someone call seeing things out of the corner of your eye. Hallucinations? Yeah, probably hallucinations. It made the most sense, anyway.

"How could you have thought everyone has that all the time?"

Laurissa furrowed her brow. Aww, she was concerned for me.

"I don't know, I guess I just never cross-referenced with anyone."

Laurissa blinked a few times. "Do you think this means I had some sort of mental illness and never realized it before?" I asked.

"It might be something serious. Maybe you should get it checked out."

"Couldn't you look at it for me?"

"I mean, I'm only a student. I don't know if I'd be able to help you or not, Olive. Don't you have a physician or a family doctor?"

"I do but I don't like to see him," I confessed. "I swear he thinks I'm psychotic."

"Well," Laurissa pointed out. "Psychosis is one of the things that causes hallucinations."

"Oh dang you're right."

"There's nothing wrong with having a psychosis," She tried to reassure me. "You just have to take care of yourself and get the proper medication, that's all. I can help if you want."

I felt good that Laurissa wanted to help me, but all the same I was really bummed. All this time, I might have been psychotic and I didn't know it.

"Then you'd be able to stop seeing Mildred so much," she offered.

I know it shouldn't have, but that idea filled me with dread. Lost Mildred? I knew she was only a figment of my imagination, but I grew attached to seeing her out the corner of my eye. I could see her running from the idea of disappearing. "Sure, I'll go see the doctor," I lied.

It wasn't like I completely dismissed the idea. I gave my decision some serious thought. On the one hand, Laurissa would be happy if I went and I could get better. On the other hand, I just didn't like the idea of losing Mildred. She's been a part of my life for so long. I laid on my bed, staring at the ceiling. Just off my vision, I could see Mildred's shadow looking at me as she faded in and out of existence. "What do I do, Mildred? I don't want to lose you. But what if something is wrong with me?"

Mildred didn't say anything.

"You're right," I replied. "If there was something wrong with me, something would have happened by now. There's nothing wrong with me, this is perfectly normal. I don't have to see any doctor. Besides, I don't have to tell Laurissa that I didn't go. I'll just tell her everything's fine. Thanks, Mildred. You're the smartest."

I never went to the doctor. Laurissa asked me how it went and I told her I was fine. I didn't want to give up Mildred, she was like a childhood friend of mine by now. It was weird, but the more I thought about it, the more of my sight Mildred seemed to cover. Perhaps I was stubborn all my life, or perhaps I've been scared from the beginning. Change is scary for anyone. The more my vision blurred, the larger the blind spot became.

I was having trouble deciphering between her and the real world for a while. I bumped into things. Laurissa asked if I was alright, and I told her I was fine. "Just dizzy is all," I told her.

By the time I realized what was going on, it was too late. Whatever I had it wasn't psychosis. More shadow chasers entered my vision. It wasn't just Mildred anymore. I finally went to the doctor once it became almost mandatory. He offered surgery, but my family couldn't afford that. I lost my sight.

It happened very quickly, too. Laurissa saw me one Friday and by Monday I was blind. I had to get a friend of mine to walk me to classrooms. It was mostly embarrassing because I had to admit to Laurissa that I lied to her. She wasn't very happy about that. She didn't talk to me much after that. Well, Mildred is still here at least.

THEY WATCH ALWAYS

This will be the last thing I will write to you. I expect to die soon. Please do not worry about me, only relay the information I'm about to give you to everyone that you hold dear to your heart.

I have deciphered the letters. At first, I started doing it in public places, but as I continued, I had begun to feel paranoid. The risks of 'agents' became a concern. Holding onto such precious information is more dangerous than it had in the past. I will attach what I had deciphered here so that what I say will make more sense.

Retrieved Note 1: There is no denying it now; the eyes are real. I have tried every coping mechanism I had ever heard or read about but nothing has worked. I don't feel dizzy and I have had plenty of sleep, good food and relaxation. Despite all my efforts the eyes of my shadow are still there, staring at me. They don't go away when I turn my head anymore. I feel them to be threatening so I do not try to look straight at them. So far, I haven't looked at them full-on. I still do not want to believe they're there, but there they are. They're watching, never blinking.

This may sound silly, but I've developed a habit of talking to my shadow. I try to ask the eyes things. 'Who are you?' 'Why are you watching me?' 'What do you expect me to do?' But I get no response. They just stare at me. Just stationary, unmoving, unblinking, unnatural eyes.

Retrieved Note 2: No matter what I try, I can't get rid of the eyes. I feel as though they're trying to drive me mad. My experiments were as follows: I tried to sit in darkness where I would have no shadow. As I did, the eyes started fading in and out of my peripheral, as though they were scrolling around the room, just out of my sight. They kept staring, urging me to look at them. I resisted, but not without losing my patience. I shouted, threw things toward them, even managed to hit them. But there was no response, no flinch of emption. Nothing changed at all.

I tried to drown out the shadow with light. I drove to the local market and bought as many high-wattage lamps as I could get. I turned on every light, and sat in the center of the room where my shadows were only slivers overlapping each other. This, to my horror, led to something worse than the darkness. My shadow hadn't been splintered; I realized dreadfully that my shadow was multiplied. Dozens, hundreds, millions of eyes were staring right at me. With me at the center, they circled me, eyes of judgment, and eyes of torment. They did not laugh or scowl, they were just emotionless eyes. They had surrounded me! In a panic I ran to the lights and turned all of the lights off. The only light that existed came through the window, and my single shadow, stronger than ever, with those two eyes.

I rearranged the lights so my shadow would be small and beneath my feet. I had a light hanging over me, but I would have to be still. Even then, it was futile. I could see the eyes staring at me from beneath my feet. I stomped on them. I cursed them! There was no response.

Retrieved Note 3: The eyes have started to multiply. I first noticed it yesterday, when I was watching television. I have been able to ignore the shadow, which led me to believe that I may be doing better. However, as I kept watching television, I saw something move out the corner of my eye, where my shadow was. I thought that at first the eyes had moved, but when I looked at them with the corner of my eye they were in the same place. I couldn't ignore the other pair of eyes, however, located on the chest of my shadow. My heart leaped, the eyes feeling like a cold grip to my spirit. They hadn't gone away. Instead of going away, there is another set now, on my forehead above the original eyes. They're all staring at me.

'It must get worse before it gets better.' I have told this to my clients for a long time. I will continue to believe this practice now as these eyes continue to collect out the corner of my eye. I can hardly see a shadow anymore, they're only eyes now.

Retrieved Note 4: My vacation was supposed to end a week ago. I extended my time both at work and told my wife. I wanted to go home, but the eyes keep multiplying. They've consumed my shadow, but I keep ignoring them. There's nothing else they can do to me now, so it's just a waiting game from here.

Retrieved Note 5: I have to get out of here. There was just recently a knock on my door. Admittedly, I was pleasantly surprised to see company. They mentioned breaking down and asked if I would come out and jump-start his car. I turned to grab my keys, but I noticed mid-way that the eyes were still there in my shadow. I turned to ask the man if he could see the eyes as well as a confirmation that I was not insane, but he was in the middle of bringing a knife down onto my head! I escaped him narrowly, but as I backed away and looked for a weapon, I had realized that his image had changed drastically. Something like black smoke was emitted from his body, and parts of him seemed blackened. Most terrifying, his eyes changed.

He came at me with the knife. I retaliated by throwing a chair at him, to buy me time. The chair hit him at first, but almost went through him as chunks of his human visage melted away. I threw everything I could find at him. He became less able to hit as time passed, becoming more like the shadow. His eyes wide and murderous, yet at the same time emotionless. His eyes were no longer like any humans. They were like the ones on my own shadow. They were surreal, almost drawn on. After a moment, he faded away, being carried away by the black smoke that engulfed him.

When he was at the door, I could have never guessed he wasn't human.

Retrieved Note 6: They're watching. Always watching. They're watching. Always watching. They're watching. Always watching. This note has eyes scribbled in pen everywhere on the page.

Retrieved Note 7: They're not just on my shadow anymore. They're not just in shadows anymore at all. They're everywhere. The eyes are covering everything. Eyes, everywhere. Nothing stops them, nothing helps. More agents of the shadow taking demons are after me. I can hear them calling my name. I have to leave here, they'll find me. I have to run. I have to go.

I keep looking at people, trying to decipher if they're an 'agent' of the eyes in the shadows. I don't think they'll come to a public place, but they could also come from anywhere. If there's anything I learned from these entries it's that these are more than just wandering eyes. They want to be secret. They must be secret. When I'm alone, my shadow already has two sets of eyes now. I know too much and they know I do. I'm going to die, soon. I'm certain they'll find a way.

But before they do, I'm leaving this information to you, so hopefully one day something can be done to stop these beings. I trust you will know what to do with this information.

So far, staying in crowded areas has been a good way to stay alive. But considering what had been done to the other cases, such as my brother, being in a crowded place also leaves you more vulnerable to the 'accidents.' If you intend to further reveal the nature of these shadow-taking eyes, be aware that they are watching you, and they will know. It's become apparent now that they will hunt you down. There are 'agents' to the eyes, but there are no traces of evidence currently on how they are formed or where they came from, or how they can take on the forms of human beings, though hopefully, and as far as we know, these forms are temporary.

The eyes begin in an individuals' shadow, but if the psychiatrist's notes are to be trusted, the eyes can end up being everywhere. There is a possibility that they do not need a shadow at all. There is a possibility that they are watching from more places than we know. I do not know why they are watching or what they want. I do not know if they're intelligent, if they speak, or even if they are the ones that cause the horrible accidents. For the last observation, however, it certainly seems as though it were the case.

I am conflicted. It may be for the best if I never spoke about these shadow-stealing eyes at all. At least then, nobody would be aware of them. There might be fewer casualties. But there is an odd feeling I get when I think about leaving this discovery alone. It's a common feeling, I think. It's wanting to figure out the puzzle. It's the desire to know the truth. I only hope that I'm not the only one that wants to find out the truth.

I hope you find this, my friend. I know that I can leave this up to you, because it is something we have in common. We have the desire to solve mysteries, no matter how strange or unsettling the target is. You have read this far, after all.

ABOUT THE AUTHOR

The stories told in this book are inspired by the dreams and memories of the author. Jean has always loved to entertain and inspire people and hopes to continue to do so with the world they've created in which these stories take place. They tell these stories believing that everything can be a learning experience and that there is always a chance to learn something new.

Printed in Great Britain
by Amazon